HUNTERS IN

THE SNOW

HUNTERS IN

THE SNOW

D. M. THOMAS

The Cornovia Press

SHEFFIELD

Published by The Cornovia Press, Sheffield, 2014

ISBN 978 1 908878 12 0 (Paperback)

ISBN 978 1 908878 13 7 (Kindle)

AUTHOR'S NOTE

This novel has evolved over many years, many transformations, and many hiatuses when I turned to writing other things, mainly poetry. I would like to thank my wife Angela for her constant encouragement to keep going with it – to the extent, at one point, of reminding me that it existed and I really should work to complete it! I am also grateful to my publisher Chris Bond, at The Cornovia Press, for his professionalism and enthusiastic personal commitment to this book.

D. M. Thomas
Truro, Cornwall

www.dmthomasonline.net

'A small landscape picture signed A. Hitler has come to light which is said to have once hung in Sigmund Freud's Viennese apartment.'

Haaretz, Israel, 2010

1

'Tell your fortune, young sir!'

I felt a bony hand grip my wrist as I was strolling, famished, through the Prater, the park noisy and gay with plump workers and their wives and girlfriends 'having a good time' on a mild early-spring Saturday evening. I could smell the dirt coming through the gaudy dress of the old gypsy, so close to me, all claws and bangles and sly ancient eyes peering up at me through her shawl. She was sitting outside her booth. I muttered 'Get off!' and tried to tear myself away. She was tenacious, but I managed to free myself, and was about to run off but she stopped me in my tracks by saying something in an unexpectedly kind voice: 'Your life is a struggle.'

I'm not used to kind voices. In Linz, perhaps, in the old days, but not here in soulless Vienna. 'Your life is a struggle,' she repeated quickly, sensing my weakness; 'I can tell that. You're in rags, you don't have enough to eat; but there's something about you, you have talents, you must write about your struggle, and your book will be famous. Here, come inside, I won't charge you; there's something about you...'

So I let myself be drawn into the murky evil-smelling booth, and sat before her. A crystal ball between us on a small table. She ignored the crystal ball but leaned forward to take my hands, palms up, in hers. Long crooked finger nails, those cheap and tawdry bangles. Her eyes closed as she seemed to go into herself, into her shawl, her thin lips mumbling incoherently. I suppose I was impressed despite myself. I know I have talents, I know there is something 'special' about me, something apart from the common herd. I also know I'm not a writer, though I have written some poems which my friend Gustl admires; but 'books', for me, at least as far as modern Vienna is concerned, suggests the degenerate, and therefore immensely popular, stories of Schnitzler and his kind.

Opening her eyes and gazing down at my palms, she now said clearly, 'I see two women in your life called Geli. Does that mean anything to you?'

Well, there is my older half-sister, Geli, and her little girl, still a toddler. Hardly two *women*, but still...it was impressive. I'm very fond of little Geli, a sweet child.

'One of them will be important in your life,' she said. 'You will love her very much; but you must be careful. It could turn out badly if you're not careful.'

I remained silent, not wishing to give anything away. She continued: 'I can see buildings; perhaps many buildings. Almost a town. It will be famous. Does that mean anything to you?'

'Well, yes. I have ambitions to be an architect. But of course no money for training, so no prospects of ever achieving my dreams.'

She gave a crooked smile, saying, 'Oh you will! The world will open up for you. These buildings, I think they could be in Poland. I see a cold landscape, I feel a bitter wind.'

'Poland!' I exclaimed. What did I want with Poland, or the Poles? Or any of those godforsaken places and races draining the lifeblood of Austria? I said aloud, 'I wouldn't want to create buildings in Poland—unless they were charnel houses!'

Letting go my hands, she spread hers and lifted her shoulders in a shrug. 'I can't help what I see. Maybe it's not Poland. I can't know everything.'

'But you think I should write about my struggling life?'

'Of course. It will be famous one day. You will be famous. I know what I see. There's something about you. One day you will remember the old gypsy woman...You are not a Jew, are you? though you look like one.'

That startled me. I know, being penniless, reliant on passed-on old kaftans from some of the Jews I mix with, in hostels or on park benches at night or selling their wares, I don't look so very different from them. I mostly leave my beard uncut, and I have—as one of the Jews said with a laugh—'desert-walking feet'. Made to look even larger by wearing cast-off boots too big for me. The kind of feet that followed Moses to the Promised Land.

'No, I'm not a Jew.'

'You worry that you might be. But I promise you you're not.'

I'm giving the impression that she spoke with perfect articulation. This was far from the case: a mix of bad German and, I assume, Romany. There were sentences whose meaning I had to guess at. As one does anywhere in Vienna—even in parliament! The obscene chaos of angry, perpetually warring minorities from every corner of our collapsing Empire. At least I could understand the gist of what the old gypsy-woman was saying. All the time her sensitive hands touching my fingers, or stroking my wrists where they emerged from my too-short, frayed coat-sleeves.

'You are troubled by what I've told you,' she said.

'No. No.' Actually I felt some relief. Though I've nothing particularly against Jews, it was good to hear her say with such assurance that I'm not Jewish. There is that rumour, whispered to me by Geli, my father's daughter by a previous marriage, that his mother had been made pregnant by her rich Jewish master, or perhaps by his lecherous son, when she was in service. He had sent her an allowance every month after the birth, so…

As though she knew my mind had wandered to my parents, the old woman half-stood, then leaned across the table to stroke my cheek almost tenderly. I winced away, fearing infection. 'You miss your mother,' she said. 'Poor boy! You loved her very much. She suffered a lot.' Tears, womanish tears, sprang to my eyes.

And of course she ended by extracting money from me! I don't know quite how it happened, but she adroitly palmed the coins meant for bread and cheese. Many a night I have sacrificed a meal for standing room at the Opera—but to have to give it up for a gypsy's ravings!

Except that, curiously, I had come to believe her. From the double name Geli, and from her air of certainty when she had expressed sympathy for losing my mother. It would not be usual for a man aged only twenty three to have lost his mother. And she had indeed suffered. Poor, dear mama, if I succeed in writing a famous book, it shall be for you.

On the way back to my lodgings, trudging through dingier and dingier streets, I tried to forget my hunger pangs by once again meditating my dream of good housing for workers and their families. Clusters of attractive two-storey buildings, each housing four families, and all around, green spaces, for playgrounds, football pitches, and so on. With railways to take the workers swiftly and conveniently to factories. A humane life!

I saw at my feet, suddenly, a little fluttering body. A bird, crippled, unable to take flight. I stooped and picked up the little terrified creature, cupped it in my hands and stroked its tiny head. Then with a quick twist I wrung its neck. I can't stand the suffering of animals.

But then, we are all animals. I can never forget my mother's animal scream when Dr Bloch pressed iodine-drenched gauze into the open cancerous wound in my mother's breast. He was doing it for the best, trying to help her, and I could see him flinch too from the pain of seeing her suffer so much. He was a kind man, who had faithfully tended to my mother when all three of my older brothers died in babyhood, one after the other. He was a Jew, but that did not bother us; he was simply the best doctor in Linz.

Arriving at the grim slum building where I was living, I heard Gustl hammering his piano from three floors below. I recognised a Brahms sonata. He plays too loudly. He's a decent pianist—as he should be since he's at a music school—but he plays too loudly. And of course that upright piano almost fills our lice-ridden, cockroach-ridden room, apart from the narrow bed, a minute table, a wooden box in one corner containing my art materials—my studio, in effect!—and two rickety chairs.

'Too loud, Gustl!' I shouted as I opened the door. 'That passage should be *cantabile*. Have you any food—I'm starving.' He stopped playing. 'There's a slice of cheese,' he said. 'In my coat pocket'. His coat was slung over a chair. I found the cheese and devoured it in three bites. Then I told him about the old gypsy, how she somehow knew mama was dead, and had died painfully; about the two Gelis. Gustl of course, being a friend from boyhood, knew all of them, and had loved my mother too.

Though of somewhat stolid, unimaginative temperament, one who surely will go on to live an uncomplicated, sensible life, he was impressed by the gypsy's powers of intuition. Especially when I added the white lie that she saw my closest friend having a fine career in music. 'Maybe I'll go and see her too,' he said.

I told him about the book she said I should write, which would be famous. Told it with a shrug and a wry smile, as if it was nonsense.

'I really think you should write it,' he said. 'After all, you've written some pretty good poems, Adi.'

'But what *kind* of book? I've no gift for making things up.'

'Well, you say she told you your life was a struggle and you should write about that. Just the truth. What happens to you.'

I said bitterly, 'Trying to sell little drawings of the Ringstrasse to buy a crust of bread!'

'It could be of interest. The kind of people you meet.' He

paused, his elbow gently resting on the piano keys, his soft hand stroking his chin. 'Life in the Vienna slums, with no money to buy shoelaces. Show the world it's not all Strauss and the Blue Danube. In fact it's the grey and muddy Danube... Apart from that—improvise.' He turned his face and body to face the keys again, and did an elaborate improvisation on the opening chords of Beethoven's Fifth. He stopped after a final thunderous chord. 'When you used to give your speeches in Linz, about art or politics, you could go on and on; it was *bravura* stuff. I envied it.'

'Books have to have order, planning.' All the same, I thought his idea worth a try.

We eventually went to bed. The little room, which had one small window we couldn't open, was stifling already in spring—just as it had been bitterly cold when we'd moved in in the winter. I tossed and turned for a long time, while Gustl was quickly asleep; at least breathing quietly. I thought about her remark that I was not a Jew. So perhaps my grand-mother, who had died untold years before my birth, had not had to suf-fer the lewd attentions of a rich Jew. Or, if she did, my father was not the consequence. The Jewish link had never been more than a whispered rumour, and I'd never believed it. All the same...

I had a horrible dream in which I was being throttled and couldn't breathe. I was shaken awake by Gustl. 'You were screaming,' he said; 'loud enough to waken the dead.'

I leapt out of bed, still feeling those strong hands around my throat, choking. I felt trapped in the cluttered airless room. I paced up and down and back, between piano and bed—only three paces before I had to turn. Back and forth, back and forth, shouting, 'People have to have air! Have to have green around them! Must be able to see some light! We must have light! This miserable, stinking city, it should be flattened—blow the whole lot to Kingdom Come!' After about ten minutes of this I'd tired myself enough to fling myself on the bed. I heard Gustl give a relieved sigh. I fixed my thoughts on the fields and hills around Linz. Gradually this calmed me and I fell asleep.

2

I disturbed Gustl's sleep three more times during the next two or three weeks, from similarly horrid dreams. And in general I did not feel well. I started to suffer from severe stomach pains and nausea. I vomited on two occasions. I began to be convinced I had something seriously wrong with me, probably a stomach cancer. I had received a small sum of money from an aunt, and was able to afford a humble meal most days; even so, there were days when I preferred to starve rather than miss an opera. I went to performances of *Lohengrin* and *The Magic Flute*. How bitter it felt to have such a devotion to music yet be unable to give it my full attention because of the gnawing stomach pains—when, in the best seats, popinjays from the Imperial Guards were lolling with their mistresses, interrupting the music with chatter and laughter!

I also heard, one Sunday afternoon, a free band concert in the Prater. The band was amateurish, but made a great din with Tchaikovsky's *1812 Overture*. It suddenly occurred to me that I could call my book, whose first few pages I had scribbled, *1912 Overture*; for if the gypsy was right, and if I was not doomed like my mother to an early grave from cancer, this was surely the overture to my life, and possibly to greatness! I felt a moment's exhilarating optimism; but a fierce stomach cramp soon put an end to it.

I took a morbid satisfaction in the sinking of the *Titanic*, cloven in two by an iceberg on its maiden voyage. The coffee-houses were buzzing with the news. Faces assumed a mask of concern and sympathy for those drowned, but beneath was a kind of delighted excitement at such a grand tragedy. My pleasure was in the overthrowing of imperialist and capitalist arrogance. It felt like the end of much more than a grandiose passenger liner on the Atlantic.

I struggled on with my drawings and paintings despite feeling ill and constantly hungry. Most days I ate only bread and butter and a small piece of seed cake, but on some days I wasn't so lucky. Then I'd sell a small watercolour for a few kronen, and could eat again. The Jewish dealers in the Leopoldstadt were often the most generous.

Around that time I had a close shave avoiding the Army draft. I had no intention of ever serving old Franz Josef and his decrepit, dying Empire. I persuaded Gustl to reply to the notice summoning me to such-and-such a barracks by saying I had left the area. I changed billets for a month with a worker who had a place at a fairly decent (as such places go) workingmen's hostel, in an area of belching factory smoke and pawnbrokers. He was a quiet, decent sort, who didn't mind Gustl's piano playing, and Gustl, for his part, probably welcomed a short break from my nightmares. I changed my name to Wolf Stiedler. Every few months I was forced to such changes, so that I scarcely knew who I was any more. My stomach continued to plague me; sleepers in adjoining cubicles complained of my waking them with screaming; and I experienced a couple of brief black-outs—fortunately when I was in my cubicle or the hostel's library.

But then, one day, it happened when I was standing amidst a gaggle of Jewish pedlars, trying to sell my postcards to the crowds milling past. It was early evening. Carriages stuffed with Vienna's rich and well-dressed rolled by, on their way to theatres, the opera, or illicit liaisons in expensive discreet restaurants. There was a chill in the air. I was tired and hungry. The hunger pangs fought a battle with nausea. I felt myself pitching to the ground; then—the next moment it seemed—I was being helped up to my feet, in a complete daze. I tried to open my eyes, but then realised, with terror, that my eyes were already open. I couldn't see a thing. I was blind. Someone shoved my hat back on my head; someone else had picked up my fallen postcards and shoved them in my ragged coat pocket. The same hands dusted me off.

In Yiddish, what I assumed was 'You alright, Wolf?'

Then I heard an unfamiliar voice, a cultivated male voice, say in German, 'Can I help? I'm a doctor.'

Yiddish again: 'He just collapsed.'

That grave, cultured voice: 'How are you, young man?'

I cried out, my voice shaking, 'I can't see! I've gone blind!'

I felt his strong hands on my shoulders, and sensed his eyes staring into mine. Then a girl's voice said, 'What do you think, father? Shall we take him home?'

'Yes. You take his other arm. Young man, what's your name?'

'Wolf. Wolf Stiedler.'

'We'll soon have you in my consulting room, where I can examine you properly. It's not far. Have you had trouble with your sight before?'

'No, never. I've blacked out before, but I could always see.'

'Then it's probably something that will pass. Some sort of migraine attack. Just walk with us, there's a good fellow.'

Helpless, I let myself be borne along; a strong man on my right, a girl on my left. On my right, the foul smell of cigar-laden clothes, on my left, the slight, pure scent of a girl's newly washed hair. But I wasn't thinking of girlish hair just then, I was in mortal fear. How could I manage without sight? This was something the gypsy had not warned me about.

I was being guided through outside tables in a narrow street. A man's voice shouted: 'Good for you, sir! They're all thieves and shysters! Teach him a lesson he won't forget!'

The girl's voice at my ear, kind, gentle: 'Take no notice. They don't realise we're Jews ourselves.'

Then we were descending a hill. Cobble stones. 'Careful here, Wolf… Here we are. There are some steps…' The girl let go my arm; I heard a heavy door being opened. The good doctor, whose grave voice reminded me of Dr Bloch's, instructed me on my steps up a marble stairway, with corners to be turned. I heard him say, 'No need to disturb the others, Anna. Straight into the consulting room.'

I was led through a long room, then the girl, Anna, opened another door and the doctor guided me in, his hand on my shoulder. I could smell richness, luxury, comfort.

'Take his coat and hat, Anna.' I unbuttoned my coat nervously, and she helped me off with it. I doffed and gave to her my hat. 'Now keep your eyes open. I'm using what is called an ophthalmoscope…'

A few highly stressful moments, then: 'I'm right. I can see nothing physically wrong with your eyes. In fact they're rather fine eyes—don't you think, Anna?' He had a smile in his voice. A good doctor's manner. She didn't respond. 'I'm sure you'll regain your sight in a short while. Maybe an hour, maybe a few.'

'But what on earth has caused it?' I burst out.

'Have you been under stress? You look gaunt. Have you eaten today?' Without waiting for an answer he said, 'Tell mama we have a young guest. He will want some food… And a bed for the night.

Young man—Wolf—you must stay here for the night.' I started to protest that I could not trouble him, but he interrupted: 'It's no trouble. My son is away at university; you can use his room. Anna, tell mama.'

I heard her footsteps run off. Her father said, 'Temporary blindness is rare, but not unheard of. It often suggests a yearning for love. But then, don't we all yearn for more of it? You probably have a little neurosis, my friend.'

'And what's that?'

'Well, I haven't the time to explain it thoroughly. A neurotic is a criminal who's not courageous enough to commit the crime.' A merry chuckle. 'Just a little joke, my friend. Everyone is neurotic. I'm neurotic, my daughter Anna is neurotic, and so are all my other children. The Pope is neurotic, Kaiser Wilhelm is neurotic—he's *very* neurotic!... It won't kill you. You see, human beings are like an iceberg; like the iceberg that killed those poor wretches on the *Titanic*...'

'Rich bloodsuckers, you mean!' I exclaimed. 'I didn't shed any tears for them.'

'Well, perhaps you're right. But an iceberg is mostly hidden beneath the waves; and so are we.'

A patter of footsteps again. 'Mother says it's fine, he can have what's left from supper.'

'Escort him to the kitchen, sweetheart.'

'Thank you, sir. You've been so kind.'

'Not at all. Goodbye.'

The girl guided me out of the consulting room, and through other halls and rooms. Such space! The warm, cosy smell of a kitchen. 'Please sit down. It's some cold sausage and coleslaw. Shall I cut up the sausage for you?'

Please.' It was humiliating.

I wolfed down the food.

'When did you last eat?'

'Two days ago.'

'Poor man!... There's a bit caught in your beard: may I?' And I felt the tickle of fingers in my beard as she retrieved the bit of sausage. The rattle of a door handle. 'Ah, papa!'

'Give him this powder to drink, Anna. He needs to sleep now. Your mother is unbelievably busy with some crocheting: could you take him to Martin's room? He can wear his nightshirt too.'

'Yes, of course.'

'Goodnight again, young man. By the way, we haven't introduced ourselves, which is very rude. My name is Freud, Sigmund Freud; though most people know me as Satan.' Another growled chuckle. 'And this is my daughter Anna. Don't worry, you'll soon have your sight back.'

'Thank you, sir.' The door closed. The apartment was very silent.

'You must have a maid to do this,' I said, as she led me out of the kitchen.

'It's her night off.'

She sat me down on a bed, and said in a matter-of-fact voice: 'Just behind your left foot you'll find a... chamber-pot.'

'Thank you.' More humiliation. She opened a drawer, and came back with a garment which she put into my arms. 'This may be too large for you, as my brother is big, but no matter. Now have a good sleep.'

'Thank you. I don't know what to say. You've been so good to me.'

'Nonsense! It's nice to be able to help one of our poor brethren from the East. We feel so sorry for them. Though you speak quite good Austrian German—you must have lived here for some time?'

'Quite some time.'

'Goodnight.' And the door closed softly. I undressed, and lay in the bed naked. It felt more luxuriously comfortable than I'd ever known a bed to be, even at home in Linz. I was asleep almost at once.

When I woke, and remembered where I was, and why I had come here, I was too frightened at first to open my eyes. When at last I did, panic choked me: I was still blind. Then, turning my eyes slightly, I saw a half-moon; then, faintly, curtains. I released a great sob of relief.

I rested, turning my thoughts over, until the depths of the night had given way to pearly morning light. Then I quickly put on my clothes. Straightening the blanket, I saw that my long, greasy hair had left a stain on the pillow. I turned it over, hoping no one would notice. While I had been sleeping someone, presumably the angelic Anna, had brought my coat and hat. I read this as a signal that they wanted me out as soon as possible. That was fine by me; I wished to escape. I opened the door and tiptoed out, and down the hall. The door to what I took to be the living-room was half-open, and there was the faint glow of lamplight. My sense of hearing still, perhaps, sharpened by temporary blindness, I heard the scrape of a pen on paper. I glanced furtively round the door—and my heart stopped. Not literally, of course, but that's an expression authors use for intense, sudden emotion. My angel of the previous night was sitting at a bureau, sideways to me, so that her face, lit up by the lamp, was in profile. And such a beautiful, truly angelic face!

- 10 -

She was in a white dressing-gown, and writing a letter. Crouched over the paper, intent, dreamy. Those fingers holding a pen, I thought, had last night touched me, even touched my beard!

I wanted to enter and burst out, 'I love you!' Or at least knock on the door gently, then enter and say, 'I can see again. I'm going now. Thank you so much and please thank your father.' I did neither. Strangled by shyness, as so often in the past, I tiptoed on, found the outside door, quietly opened it and went running down the marble stairs.

3

When, some weeks later, I was back living with Gustl, the lice and the cockroaches, I showed him shyly what I had written. I had never spoken to him of my fearsome attack of blindness, to make my written account the more dramatic when he should read it.

'What an amazing experience!' he said, when he had finished. 'Is that just how it happened?'

'Of course. You said to write the truth.'

'The truth, the whole truth and nothing but the truth. Some of the grammar and spelling aren't too good, but that's what editors are paid for. You should change the names. Authors do that, in case they're sued. You can use mine, of course. I've nothing to hide, and I won't sue you!...

'If you do, make sure your lawyer is a Jew!'

'Are there any other? Just be careful, that man is notorious; he'd wrap your guts around your neck.'

'Don't worry; I've no intention of writing anything bad about him. He was kind. In any case, I'll muddle and confuse everything.'

He nodded. 'Just like you muddled and confused old Frau Schmidt in her shop.'

I chuckled at the memory. A gaggle of us boys, pretending to buy underwear for our mothers and sisters.

'So you fell in love, Adi!'

'Yes. But I'm afraid it's hopeless.'

'I don't see why. Girls like you. You might have had Klara if only you weren't so shy.'

Klara was a beautiful girl in Linz, whom I would gaze at adoringly when she took the evening walk through the main street. All the citizens paraded in their finery. She was always with either her parents or some peacock of an officer, and I lacked the courage to make myself known to her. Gustl says she was aware of me, and longed for me to make an approach. But I was too poor, I couldn't compete with the Imperial pop-injays. Once, just once, I bought a lottery ticket, and I convinced myself that I would win the main prize. Then I would build a palatial villa that I could take her to, and it would make her love me and share her life with me. I drew elaborate plans for our villa. To my intense surprise and dis-may I didn't win the lottery.

Klara's image had come with me to Vienna, and when I watched and listened to *Tristan and Isolde*, superbly conducted by Gustav Mahler in my first year in the capital, it was Klara and I singing the great love-duet. Only now, five years later, had her image withdrawn in favour of this new, still brighter angel of purity.

'Who is Klara?' I said.

But now to take you back in time, so that you, my future reader, can as it were catch up with Gustl's reading… On the day after my flight from the good doctor's apartment, I was sitting in the hostel library, reading the poet Heine and, between stanzas, daydreaming about this new love in my life. For a workers' hostel, it was a rather decent library, divided into Smoking and Non-smoking; though of course the stench from the other side of the screen would drift across. There was one old man often there, smoking his stinking pipe. It reminded me of papa's pipe, stinking our house out. When he died I wanted to get rid of it, but mama, cher-ishing his memory—God knows why—kept it in his rack. For her it was sacred, 'Uncle's pipe'. She always called him Uncle. Well, that made sense—he *was* her uncle. Or much-older cousin. The family lines were very confused and mixed up.

But anyway—as I sat there that afternoon, the pipe-smoker was absent; the air was pure; pure like my thoughts of love, of Anna.

The janitor, a bald, surly fellow, stuck his head around the door. 'There's a young lady wants to see you, Stiedler. Says her name's Anna.'

I leapt up, my heart thumping joyfully. 'Oh, let her in!'

'Not really allowed, you know that. Don't seem your sort. Swanky. Alright—but no going upstairs.'

He withdrew, and a few moments later I heard her gentle voice saying 'Thank you', and then she appeared in the doorway, smiling at sight of me. Only she wasn't the same girl I'd glimpsed writing a letter under lamplight; not that angel, that beauty. This girl was plain, and younger. A mere schoolgirl of sixteen or seventeen, carrying a satchel.

'Wolf! May I come in?'

My mind was racing. A sister. Obviously. 'Yes,' I muttered, trying not to scowl. I sat and she sat opposite me. The smile never left her face.

'Your sight is back! What are you reading?' She grabbed my book and turned it towards her. 'Heine! Oh, I love him! Fancy you reading poetry! And Heine, our great Jewish German poet.'

'And why shouldn't I?' I said aggressively.

'Oh, no reason. Sorry.'

And then I said 'Sorry' because I farted, loudly, involuntarily. My stomach was very bad. But in a way it expressed my feelings. 'How did you find me?'

'I asked some of the others on the bridge. We were worried about you, Wolf. Why on earth did you rush out so early, and without telling us you were alright?'

'If I hadn't been alright I wouldn't have been able to leave, would I?' I realised I was being bad-tempered and ungrateful, and added more softly, 'I didn't want to trouble your family any more. You were very kind. You shouldn't have come here, though, a decent girl like you. The streets are very rough around here.'

She gave a little shudder, and nodded; she ran a hand over her white blouse, as if wiping off dirt; then said the hostel was unexpectedly nice. She looked around. 'And clean.'

I was conscious *I* wasn't particularly clean, and recalled the stain my greasy hair had left on the pillow. Her brother's pillow when he was at home *on vacation*. From university. My God! A mere technical school for me. 'It's not bad,' I said, 'as these places go; but it's not a real home; not like yours. You're lucky, Fräulein.'

'Call me Anna—please… I know I am.'

'You and your parents and brother. And sisters?'

Her eyes moved aside, the smile faded. 'One sister at home. Sophie.' I saw from her reaction she was jealous. Jealous of her loveliness. As how shouldn't she be?

'So are you well, Wolf? You look very pale.'

Pain griping me at that moment, I told her I suffered acutely with my stomach. She screwed up her eyes and nodded sympathetically. As if prompted by my tale of stomach misery, she opened her satchel and took out a small brown parcel. 'I know you don't eat enough,' she said. 'It's just some cheese and an apple. It's the remains of my lunch. Please take it. I hate to see food wasted.'

I pushed the parcel away. 'I don't want charity.'

'It's not charity.'

'Did you feed me sausage that night?'

'Yes,' she said, puzzled. 'You know I did.'

'I wouldn't have eaten it if I could have seen it. It looks like shit.'

Her colour blenched; her lips parted in a gape. I immediately stammered an apology. 'It's just that I find the *idea* of eating animals revolting. I detest cruelty to animals—can't bear it. I would like to be a vegetarian. I have little money for food anyway. But if you are starving you have no choice... You were very kind. Please thank your father again on my behalf. And now you must go. Before it gets dark. They kidnap girls around here, and ship them off to brothels in Rio de Janeiro. Keep to the sunny, light side of the road. Run past the pawnbrokers' dens. Hurry home! Hurry home!'

With a dazed look, as if she couldn't decide what manner of man I was, she stood up. I went with her to the library door, caught hold of her limp hand and pressed it to my lips. 'Take care, Anna.'

4

This brief intrusion of the plain sister did not in any way interfere with my vision of the beautiful sister. On the contrary, she lived in my imagination all the more powerfully. For a time I could think of nothing else. Having sold not a single picture, I would turn my steps to that part of the Leopoldstadt district, where Jews are congregated, to the cobbled hill where I was sure she lived, and I would wander up and down it hoping for a glimpse of her. She never appeared. I began to think, despairingly, that she had gone forever. Like Klara in Linz. (I had heard that Klara had married one of the military peacocks.)

The Heine that the wrong Freud girl had found me reading did not occupy me for long. Poetry has only a limited value in the great scheme of things. But I have always loved literature, and from my earliest days I have read voraciously. Making use of libraries, for of course there was never any money to buy books. The library at my temporary refuge, the workingmen's hostel, was in fact, as I have remarked, quite decent, and I made full use of it. For instance, in only one week I read Cervantes' *Don Quixote*, Dante's *Inferno*, Shakespeare's *Hamlet* and a book about the lives of the great artists. All this in addition to my other activities and while not feeling well. I burned the midnight oil.

The idea that I would never again be able to read had been one of the worst horrors of blindness. Finding my sight restored led me to devour books all the more eagerly.

Among the books in the library I found one by Dr Freud. I had known of him, even before our encounter, as a doctor who had joined the crowded ranks of the controversialists and dissenters busily stirring the stewpot of unrest. I had never read a word by him. So when I found his book, which fell open at pages where there was some lurid material of a sexual nature, I immediately settled to read it. It purported to be a series of 'case studies' in which Dr Freud had treated a patient for some distressing symptom, such as partial paralysis or complete loss of voice. Traditional medicine such as the use of hydro-electric shock, he claimed, had failed them. They were considered 'incurable'. That word always made my hackles rise. It had been used of my mother. It only meant *they* could not cure it! Politicians say the same thing: we can't cure the ills of society! Well, I always think, try harder, you scoundrel! Or pass the task on to someone else, with fresh ideas!

Once these patients came to Dr Freud, a miraculous cure would take place. Much I could not follow, not from lack of intelligence or concentration, but because of the jargon, the gibberish, he made use of. I had to read much more slowly than usual. But it soon became apparent that the key to the patient's miraculous recovery was a dream of some kind. It might be a very ordinary dream, like buying two hats for a wedding because the woman (almost all the patients were female) couldn't decide between them; but Freud would question her until, lo and behold, the dream somehow revealed that the patient was in love with the bridegroom, wished she were marrying him instead of his actual bride; being unwilling to face up to her shameful desire she had found her arm or leg paralysed (or whatever her problem was). As soon as Freud made her face up to it, the problem either vanished completely or was greatly eased. Dr Freud was the modern version of Jesus Christ—'Take up thy bed and walk'!

Sometimes a slip of the tongue could reveal the answer to this miracle man. He would seize on a very normal verbal mistake and prove that the patient hated her husband and wished him dead, or perhaps had never recovered from having seen her parents performing the sexual act. Some of Freud's twistings made me chuckle out loud, bringing a 'shush' from the man overseeing us.

In short, I thought Dr Freud was a mountebank, a quack. And lewdly over-sexual. The women he treated were all rich, members of the bourgeoisie, otherwise they would never have been able to pay his fees, which I was confident were extremely high. These wealthy, spoiled ladies had too much time on their hands, too little to do. They had servants to cook and clean, nannies or governesses to look after their children, husbands who bothered them very little, either because they were working all hours, probably exploiting slave labour, or visiting their mistresses—or more likely both. The ladies' minds were too small to engage in meaningful, creative activity, so they dwelt on their physical symptoms and made mountains out of molehills.

No, I decided very quickly, Dr Freud, though I was very grateful to him for his attention to me, had nothing to offer to the toiling masses. Nothing to the men I saw around me in the hostel who came back drained from twelve hours of backbreaking labour. I had read his book in a couple of hours—then joined in a rowdy evening argument about Jews. Fists were not flying but voices were high and threatening; some of my Jewish acquaintances were under attack and I flew to defend them, leaping on a table to harangue the company about the need to be decent to each other. We had the common bond of poverty, I told them—reducing them to silence. That was real life! a good brawl about vital, bread-and-butter issues.

But underlying all this was the vision of Sophie. She did not fade with time. I kept seeing, first thing in the morning and last at night, that pure, radiant face bent over a letter she was writing.

But it seemed hopeless, like Quixote for his Dulcinea. I kept haunting the Berggasse whenever I could spare an hour, hoping to catch sight of her. I never did. She must either be a complete stayathome or I was just unlucky in the times I could visit. I had a second reason for going there—to show some dealers pictures, and I did sell a couple to long-bearded, side-locked gentlemen. This consoled me but little. Was Sophie to be another dream (not in Dr Freud's sense of the word) doomed to wither? It seemed so.

I heard that the famous German adventure-story writer and idealist, Karl May, was to give a lecture in Vienna. I became tremendously excited. His stories about the American Wild West, and cowboys and indians, obsessed me in childhood. I am no longer a lover of exotic fantasies, but a lecture by him, now an old and sick man, simply could not be missed.

I worried that he would not get a good audience, since it had recently been revealed that he had been imprisoned for theft and fraud in his youth—and moreover had never set foot in the distant countries he wrote about in the first person! That didn't in the least surprise me; I thought, why *should* he have done? Had Dante visited Hell? Had he bumped into Beelzebub and Moloch, and been shown the torture devices? I doubted it. As for theft and fraud—well, what rich Jew in Germany or Austria (which I believe are the same thing) has not been guilty of the same offences!

To my relief, when I arrived at the Sophie Halls—oh, what a

romantic pang that name now gave me!—with a couple of others from the hostel, I could see it was crammed full; there must have been at least three thousand there, and everyone of them worried that their besmirched hero would be badly received! When he appeared, he was cheered to the rafters by his vast audience of women, petit bourgeois workers and boys. A dapper, somewhat old-fashioned figure: white curly hair and pince-nez, a cheerful, almost boyish, smile. Aged seventy, and scarcely recovered, according to reports, from pneumonia, he looked extremely shaky, but lectured with zest.

He spoke of the nobility of pacifism; how man would progress, through higher and higher spheres, to a realm of justice and peace. He read passages from his books to illustrate his theme; and all around me I could see eyes shining and heads lifting. I could feel a glimmer of tears in my eyes, and noticed them in others'. I felt it was just a pity that one cannot see much nobility or peace in our city outside the Sophie Halls— merely insults and fists swailing between Germans and Czechs, or Serbs and Poles and Hungarians, or all against the Jews: even brawls in parlia- ment!

When he tottered from the stage, to tumultuous applause, my companions and I waited patiently enough for our turn to leave—yet still had to push and jostle to prevent others from shoving past us to the doors. A man's elbow poked my side, hurting me. When I muttered 'Ouch!' he merely scowled, as if it was my fault. So much, I thought, for universal peace and the noble human being! Once we were outside, in the warm dusk, we found our way still blocked by the huge numbers who were waiting for the great man to appear.

I felt a hand touch my shoulder, and turned to find myself looking straight into the eyes of Anna Freud. Her eyes were glowingly alive. 'Fräulein! Fancy seeing you here!' She replied, 'I wouldn't have missed him for the world. I love his books. Wolf, this is Sophie, my sister. Sophie, you recall we told you about Wolf, our overnight guest a couple of weeks ago?'

That unexpected sight of her again overwhelmed me. I dropped my gaze, too shy to confront Sophie's eyes direct. I held out my hand and she took it. Limply.

'Wasn't he brilliant?' Anna exclaimed. 'So inspiring! I've read all his books; they uplift the spirit.' Politely I introduced my companions, two other long-bearded eastern Jews. I say 'other' loosely, as it were through the Freud girls' eyes, since I looked little different in my kaftan. At that moment a great roar went up, and we saw the frail old yarn-spinner standing on the steps above us, flanked by two of the organisers. May doffed his hat and jiggled his pince-nez in appreciation. I clapped my hands above my head and huzza'd. The old man started to descend, cautiously, totteringly, his arms grasped by his helpers. A corridor opened up for them in the throng, and we could see them no more. We waited as everyone started to move away slowly.

'I didn't know till tonight he was blind for the first five years of his life,' Anna said. 'What he had to surmount! What a man!'

'Yes,' I said, 'I experienced it for a few hours. That was enough. What a man!'

The Jewish workers moved off, nodding politely at the two young ladies. 'They have to get back, they're working night-shift in a boot factory,' I explained. 'I should go with them, it's a long walk, but I feel restless, I don't want to lose that rapture just yet, as I would be bound to in my hostel room. Also, on the way they would engage me in small-talk. They're nice fellows, but tonight I need to be in a different realm, with people of idealism and intellect; even if that means being with myself.'

'I feel the same,' Anna said; 'how can one talk about trivia, after listening to that! Can it really be that we're on the verge of a universal and everlasting peace?'

'That's just as likely as... well, papa learning to play tennis!' said Sophie, and she threw her head back in a merry laugh. Her eyes sparkled; she was entirely enchanting.

'But his optimism is infectious,' Anna countered. 'He makes you feel it could be possible. If there is justice first. Didn't you love it when he said...' I can't remember what; my gaze was only for Sophie, turning up her collar and shivering against the chill evening. I wanted to offer her my ragged long coat, warm her, hold her, create a splendid villa for her.

Her sister brought me down to earth by asking how my health was. Had I suffered any more attacks?

I decided to be honest. To attract Sophie's pity? I don't know. 'I've not been blind again, but I've had a couple of black-outs, some dreadful nightmares, stomach problems a-plenty.' It was true enough. I still believed I had stomach, or possibly brain, cancer.

'I'm sorry.' She touched my arm.

'Fräulein, I feel I was somewhat rude to you when you visited the hostel. You were so kind, and I spoke in a surly way. Would you and your sister do me the honour—would you allow me to...' I trembled and stammered, having to jerk my words out. 'No, it's impossible; why should two such refined girls as you consent to any such thing!'

'Any such what?' Sophie said.

'Allow me to buy you a cup of coffee. No, you see, it's absurd! Forget I spoke; I'll be off.' And I doffed my black hat.

'Wait!' Anna grabbed my arm. 'We'd love to, wouldn't we, Sophie?'

She looked doubtful; no, positively reluctant. 'It's late.'

'Oh, go on!' her sister said. She now squeezed Sophie's arm.

'Alright. That's kind. Thank you.'

I had the feeling she was being 'sensitive'—to a poor pedlar, a dirty smelly Ostjew. But even if so, that was alright. Just to be with her. I knew I could charm girls. We set off walking, I continuing to express my approval of May's utopian ideals and exchanging with Anna opinions on his various books. I led them to a comfortable café down a side-street and found a corner table. For a while there was an uneasy silence, the subject of Karl May having been temporarily exhausted. Awkward, I stared at the floor. To be more accurate, I stared at my feet. Those desert-walking feet. Though I noticed that Anna's would be quite good for desert-walking too.

Our coffees arrived. We sipped them. I gazed at Sophie. She seemed to warm to me, smiling, even chuckling at a joke. Rising above the hum of conversation around us, the unmistakable noises of a political demonstration, in a street not far away. Slogan-chanting, shouts, a cry of pain from some blow with a fist or stick. It's all too familiar, almost impossible to avoid anywhere in Vienna, and no one in the café takes any notice. What they *do* notice, quite clearly, are the two genteel but shameless German-Austrian girls talking to this down-at-heels, long-bearded Jewish apparition. I felt those thumping sounds, those cries of pain, seep into my bones, stir in my stomach. 'There's so much violence,' I said; 'May's pacifism must be right. People learn violence at home. My father used to beat me, when he came home drunk. And he'd call out the number of the blows.' I waved my arm in a thrashing motion: 'Thirteen, fourteen, fifteen—beat! beat! beat!'

I saw their eyes widen in horror; Anna's especially. Good!—if only she would leave. 'Mama would try to protect me, but then he'd beat her.'

'How terrible!' Anna said.

'But he had his comeuppance—a stroke when he had drunk too much.' I said that I'd been reading Dante's *Inferno*, and learned from it that the punishment fits the crime. I could see both girls were impressed by this illustration of the breadth of my reading. I added that it was important to draw out the essence from a great work of literature, such as 'to be or not to be' from *Hamlet*.

At nearby tables I could see glances over shoulders, followed by lowered, disapproving voices. Sophie, her elbows on the table, leaned closer to me, as if to rebuke the anti-Semites, but also I felt because she really liked me. It was enough for one evening. 'I'd better get back to the hostel,' I said. 'I'll just go and pay.'

Sophie started to say, 'No, please, let us'—but her sister touched her arm and shook her head slightly. I knew she was saying, His pride wants to pay for this. She said, aloud, smiling at me: 'Papa was right. You really do have fine eyes. Are they blue, are they green, are they grey? A little of all of them. Don't you think so, Sophie?'

The lovely, pure vision, resting her chin on her clasped hands, simply smiled and gave me—extraordinarily—a wink! It was saying, 'She's keen on you, and thinks you feel the same towards her; but *we* know, don't we?'

My heart sang with joy as I trudged my lonely way 'home'; but then sank as I wondered if I would see her again. And the following days were a desert, a desert without a Promised Land at the end.

5

I had returned to live with Gustl. One cloudy, cold day I was standing outside the Opera, offering my postcards showing drawings of it to passers-by, and having no luck. Suddenly Anna, in her school uniform, breathing heavily, her cheeks glowing, stood before me, smiling. 'So *there* you are, Wolf! Your friends told me to look here or outside parliament.'

'Oh, hello.'

Her face saddened. She said, 'Karl May has died; his visit to Vienna was too much for him; he developed pneumonia again. I wanted to let you know.'

'I already read it in the newspapers,' I said. 'It's sad.'

'Yes, so sad. How have *you* been?'

'Not very well. My stomach hurts; I think it was caused by a blow from some oaf's elbow after May's lecture; it might even have started a cancer. Yesterday I suffered another black-out; but fortunately I was with my room-mate. He's very long-suffering—I keep waking him with my screams, when I have nightmares.'

'I'm really sorry. But I have some good news. Papa has agreed to see you again, treat you for whatever is causing these… these neurotic problems, and for free!'

'I don't want charity.'

She said he had a social conscience, and if he liked someone, as he liked me, he was more than happy to treat him for free, and make it up by over-charging the rich. 'You'll just have to *talk*, about anything that comes into your head.'

'I've read about what he does. It seems nonsensical.'

'Well, it isn't! He's cured lots of people. Come on Monday evening. And have a bit of supper after. Please...'

I said yes; not because of the supper or least of all the 'treatment', which I knew would be a complete waste of time, but because I would be near Sophie and would surely see her. It was a golden opportunity, well worth the tedium of sessions with her father.

Dr Freud shook my hand, then indicated a sofa with cushions and a richly coloured blanket.

'Please lie there.'

I remembered only the rich, musty smell of this room, but now saw it was cluttered with small sculptures, statuettes, many behind glass. 'I'd rather sit.'

'Well, that's alright. You're not paying for this; if you were paying, I'd *order* you to lie flat!' He chuckled and sat down in a curiously shaped chair, like a pharoah's throne. I sprawled on the sofa. He lit a cigar. Foul!

Several minutes' silence followed. Finally, overcome by boredom, I said, 'Shouldn't you be asking me questions?'

Ash from his cigar fell on the carpet. 'No. If you were paying me, I might feel obliged to; but you're not, so it's up to you!'

Somewhat histrionically I leapt to my feet, waving my arms, and began to march up and down the room, like a conductor who has lost his orchestra. 'You insult me, sir! You are making me aware, all too clearly, that I am poor.'

'Sit down, please.'

Having made my point, I sat back down, wearing a sulky expression.

'I didn't mean to insult you, Wolf; I don't regard money as an indication of a person's worth. It's late in the day, when normally I relax with a walk. I can see how you might have taken it amiss and I'm sorry... Tell me what was in your mind while we were silent.'

I said I had had no particular thoughts—just melodies from *Lohengrin* going round in my head. He confessed that music had more or less passed him by, and that the only operas he liked were Mozart's.

'*Figaro* is wonderful,' I agreed, 'but nothing matches the sublime power of Wagner. Last night was pure bliss—or would have been, except for the boorish chattering of the officers. They're only waiting for the interval, when they can pay court to women. And yet they're admitted for ten hellers—twenty times less than we poor people, we real music-lovers, have to pay!'

- 24 -

'You're not fond of the military.'

'I loathe them! I'm a pacifist.' He nodded, and waited. After a time I said, 'But I will not allow those military morons to overwhelm the beauty of the music. Although the performances I recall with most ecstasy were those under the baton of Gustav Mahler. I came to Vienna four—no, five—years ago, and had the privilege of attending a few of his productions before he was forced to resign.'

'I knew him quite well,' Dr Freud said. 'I did my best to prevent him from resigning. It was anti-Semitism, of course.'

'Stupid! He was a great conductor.'

Well, this chatter was easy enough. My stomach rumbled and I looked forward to some food, and wondered if Sophie was at home. I heard him ask if I myself was a musician. No, I responded, though I can play the piano a little, and had been trained as a chorister in a Benedictine monastery in childhood. The music, together with the architectural splendour of the building, had inspired me. I was attempting to compose an opera about Wieland the Smith, having heard that Wagner had left some fragments on that subject at his death. With the help of a music student who kept a piano in our bug-ridden room, I was slowly putting the opera together.

This was not true, I was improvising, the idea had been barely a glimmer until now; but as I said it I became excited at the thought of composing an opera. 'I have the whole opera in my head!' I exclaimed enthusiastically. 'Of course it's hard, we neither of us have enough technical knowledge; and even if we did I couldn't hope to match Wagner.'

'But you'd come close?' he asked, tipping off more ash.

'Possibly.' But my main ambitions, I said, lay in the direction of architecture. I had great plans for transforming Vienna. During the course of several minutes I outlined my dreams for the city—once jumping up again, gesticulating, before throwing myself back onto the sofa. I would, I told him, sweep away all the insanitary, spirit-and-body-destroying tenements, and create green spaces each side of the Danube. I would build human-sized houses for the workers, just two-storeys high, each with ample accommodation for four families, and surrounded by gardens. Each cluster of units would be surrounded by wider patches of green, and have their own school, shops, playing field, concert hall and so on; linked to their places of work in the city by railway lines. The spirit of the people would flower.

When at last I had finished speaking, I noticed that his cigar had gone out and he had not bothered to re-light it. He reflected for awhile, hand stroking his short beard; then said, 'I wish you luck with your plans.' His eyes twinkling: 'But do you think they are a trifle too ambitious for a young man? Maybe start by demolishing just one tenement block rather than all Austria?'

'No! you have to be radical! That's the only way.' I slammed a fist into one of the cushions. 'The whole earth if necessary.'

'Maybe you're right. Radical surgery.'

'That's what *Wieland the Smith*, my opera, is going to be about— smashing the whole hideous so-called civilisation the capitalists have created, and starting afresh! But I have no money, no training, no prospects. I'm going to have to make my own way. That's why I must regain my health. I know I'm not strong. Last night it was all I could do to stand through *Lohengrin*, and of course I can't afford a seat. If only I could find a sweet Jewish wife, from a family with money and ideals and a belief in my talents, there's no telling where I might go, what I might become...'

'Could you perhaps tell me more about *your* family background?'

'I don't see how that's relevant. You wouldn't ask'—I searched for a suitable parallel—'Jesus about his family background!'

'Why not? It would be interesting,' he replied drily. 'I'd love to know more about that curious *ménage à trois*, the Christian Father, Son and Holy Ghost! But you're not Jesus, you're a young Austrian German Jew, I take it. So tell me about your family, please.'

How tedious. What does one's family background matter? 'Both my parents are dead. Father was a Customs official, working on and around the border between Austria and Germany. They were in Braunau am Inn when I was born. He was already quite old. Upon retirement, he moved us to Linz. Well, *finally* to Linz; he liked to move house quite a lot. He changed wives quite a lot too! As a young man he married a woman of fifty. I don't know much about her, except she objected to one of the servant girls, who became too close to father, if you know what I mean...'

'I think so! And how did his wife express her objection?'

'She got a separation. Then died soon after, and father married this servant and had two children by her. Then *she* didn't like my father's niece coming to help out in the house... that was my mother...'

His grave head jerked up. 'Your mother? Your mother was your father's niece?'

'Yes. Father was kind to her. He'd welcomed her into his home earlier, as a young girl, when he was with his first wife. *She* threw her out too.'

His head dropped again. 'Jealousy, lots of jealousy... A malady most incident to wives... Go on.'

I made my voice grow slightly husky. 'It's awful to think of her being thrown out for no reason, twice. My mother would *never* have done anything wrong. She came back again when father's second wife fell ill and needed nursing; also of course to help with the children. That wife died too, and my mother and father married. He was too old for her; with a moustache like Franz Josef's, and pomposity to match. Very aware of his dignity. Though this didn't stop him going to the tavern every day—and that's where he died. In a tavern.'

'How old were you then?'

'Fourteen.'

'When our fathers die, it's a momentous event. We step up to the front line, so to speak; and you were very young when that happened to you. It must have left you shaken up for a long time.'

'Well, I burst into tears when I went to the tavern to help bring his body home. But I got over it quickly. I respected him, I didn't love him. He was very stern. My older half-brother ran away from home at fourteen, because he didn't like being thrashed so much; then I took his place. But what is the point of—?'

'He beat you?'

'Often. I can hear him now, counting out the blows... Twenty eight, twenty nine, thirty, thirty one, thirty two... The whip coming down on me... Look, I'm a little disturbed by that Roman figure up there, the woman with her robes clinging to her boyish shape...'

'That's called the Gradiva,' he said. 'Go on.'

'—She is so like my mother, my beloved mother.' My voice—this time unintentionally—broke on the last word. 'Her figure, her features, even the plaits around her forehead...'

'She was young of course, when you first knew her.' His voice seemed to tremble a little at this.

'Oh, yes. She was only in her forties when she died, four years ago. She didn't have much of a life. I don't know what she expected from marrying father; probably little, but what she found was less than that, I imagine. She was frightened of him—and frightened for me. She never stopped calling him Uncle.'

'Uncle, h'mm? An odd form of address for one's husband!'

'Yes. Before I came along, mama gave birth to three little children; but in the space of a few weeks they all died, in an outbreak of diphtheria.'

Ah, that's sad.'

'Then after me, there was Edmund, who died at six. And finally a girl, my sister Paula, who's a bit stupid. Poor mama…'

'Lots of dead wives, and dead children…' He pulled out his watch. 'It's time. I've a paper to write. Go and have some food, young man! You've done well.'

'I don't know what good this has'—

'—Of course you don't! Neither do I, right now. But I shall find out later. Oh, and by the way, try to smarten yourself up. It helps our mental health to look smart. I can see you do your best to keep your clothes darned, but probably you have to hack your beard around yourself… We've had liver dumpling soup for supper, and it's good! Our maid will serve you. And come again on Thursday, same time… Try and remember your dreams.'

Besides the maid in the kitchen there was the mother-figure, stately, plain and taciturn; and Anna came in and asked me how it had gone. I had three bowlfuls of the liver dumpling soup. No Sophie, to my sorrow.

For my next visit I changed my appearance radically. Short hair; practically clean-shaven, a new second-hand coat. I had done a deal with a Jewish barber—a couple of nice watercolours for his work on my appearance and the coat.

'My God!' the good doctor said, after the maid had shown me in. 'You look practically like a *goy*! And doubtless you feel better for it.'

'I'm afraid not. Another black-out, and vomiting… But I do remember one dream…' Gustl and I had made it up, laughing uproariously.

'Good! Tell it to me. But first, tell me where your mother and father came from, originally.'

'I don't know about originally.'

'No, of course. Probably some unknown *shtetl* in Galicia.'

Probably, I agreed. But so far back as family memory went, they belonged to the Waldviertel. Land of stubborn peasants, harsh soil for farming, bleak hills and woods, dire poverty, superstition.

'Border country,' the doctor observed. Close to Bohemia. It's perhaps not surprising your father worked in the Customs service.'

He had to fight his way up,' I said with a little pride. 'He only went to elementary school, but reached the equivalent rank to an army captain.'

'He did well, he did well. He must have wanted you and your brother to rise even higher.'

'He wanted me to be a civil servant like him. Boring, boring, boring!'

'Well, I can sympathise. Now let's hear this dream.'

'You were in it, Dr Freud, and you weren't much use then either! Yes, how astonishing! I'm sorry, I don't see how dreams can help. They're just bits and pieces left over from the previous day, I've found. Oh, well! Let me try to remember...' I gave my smooth chin a stroke. 'There was a river. I could choose which side I'd live on. You were a ferry-man in a rowing boat. You kept rowing me from one side to the other. I couldn't make up my mind; because you told me once I set foot on shore I'd have to stay there. On one side it was snowing. I don't like it when it snows; I hate winters. Too much death in winter. On the other side it wasn't snowing, though the sky was grey. There was some unknown man there called Herr Hakenkreuz. He kept waving at me impatiently to step ashore. But on the other side, the snowy side, were my mother and Edmund—my younger brother who died. Mother was trying to call out something to me, but I couldn't hear. I woke up, still without having made up my mind where to live, but with a line of the poet Heine in my head. What was it?... Something about sleep... "Sleep is so good, but death is better." Yes, that's it. Perhaps that's what mama was trying to tell me.'

He was gaping, his cigar held out. I could see he was fascinated. After a few moments he said, 'You were born in Braunau am Inn, and presumably almost every day your father had to cross the river from Austria into Germany and back.' I nodded agreement enthusiastically. 'The border river,' he mused.

'But I was only three when we left.'

'That doesn't matter. Your unconscious has stored it up... Then there's the mysterious Herr Hakenkreuz—the whirling cross common in Eastern religions, the Swastika...'

'I know that! I'm not ignorant!' I burst out. 'It was carved on the gateway and four corners of the Abbey at Lambach, where I went to school and sang in the choir. I liked being there. For a time I wanted to be a monk or a priest. Mama was very religious; she'd have liked that.'

'So you were tempted, Wolf, to land on the side where Herr Hakenkreuz stood.'

'I was. But you see'—I made my voice choke slightly—'mama was on the other side, also calling me. And little Edmund. Well, of course, it's a distorted memory of the day Edmund was buried. It was snowing then too. Geli, my older half-sister, and I were alone in the cemetery saying goodbye to him; it was a dreadful day.' I curled up miserably.

'You were alone with your half-sister? Where were your mother and father?'

'I don't know!' I spoke the words almost with a howl. Almost a wolf's howl. 'They went off somewhere.'

'Perhaps your mother couldn't stand it, after all the other deaths.'

'Perhaps... And it was winter when she died too. Christmas Eve! We had a Christmas tree with all the lights! Now I can't stand Christmas.'

I blinked rapidly several times, as if to ward off tears. Then I really did have a lump in my throat.

'You loved your little brother.'

'Yes, yes I did. Oh, of course we quarrelled.'

'And of course you were a bit jealous of him, coming along and taking a lot of your mama's attention. Sibling rivalry is very frequent, natural indeed. You should just see my daughters, Sophie and Anna!' He chuckled.

Then I burst out: 'That's it! It's no mystery why I dreamed of a river and a ferry. I'd been reading "The Lay of Hoar-beard"—that's a poem in the Edda'

'Ah! I'm not too familiar with the Edda.'

'There's a grey-bearded ferryman, perhaps Odin or Loki, who forbids the crossing to Thor, making him go the long way round. And I remember, while reading, a grey mood coming over me when the ferryman tells Thor his kinsfolk are in mourning, because his mother has died. And Thor says something like "those are the worst words a man can hear." That's why I dreamt of a river and a ferry, and my mother, and graves—there's no need to go hunting for hidden meanings!'

Gently he rebuked me. Why had my unconscious mind chosen just that impression, out of a thousand and one impressions from my recent past? 'I suspect it's a very significant dream, Wolf. River-crossings by ferry represent a voyage to some new state: perhaps a state of greater wisdom, perhaps death. You have heard of Charon and the Styx, I dare say.'

'Of course.'

'The difference here is, Which side are you coming *from*?'

'I don't know. I'm just on the ferry, being rowed to and fro. And you are no help, ferryman!' I summoned up a sarcastic smile.

'We must find out who this Herr Hakerkreuz is.'

'I sold a small watercolour a few days ago of the Abbey, basing it on a picture postcard. It reminded me of the carvings. Again this is shit!'

Looking 'wistfully' up at the Roman lady, I said, 'Mother would not like to hear me use coarse words.'

'That sentence from the Norse lay—"the worst words a man can hear"... did you get word of your mother's death while you were here, in Vienna?'

'No, thankfully I was at home in her last weeks, after she wrote to me saying she was not quite so well. That was the phrase she used—not quite so well! I rushed back to Linz to be with her, and found her, oh so changed, so thin, tortured by pain—dying! She had breast cancer; a breast had been removed and I'd gone off to Vienna thinking she was on the mend; and for a few months she was able to shop and cook and look after my little sister. I felt content that we had a wonderful family doctor, Dr Bloch, who was known throughout Linz as "the people's doctor", he was so kind. Even though he is Jewish, and Linz people are quite anti-Semitic, everyone praised him. But then, after she got worse again and I came back, he said to me one day, "I'm afraid it's incurable."'

I sprang up from the sofa and strode around the room agitatedly, gripping my fists tight. I shrieked out, 'Incurable! What do they mean by incurable? It just means *they* don't know how to cure it!'

I flung myself down again, breathing deeply and rapidly. When I had calmed a little, I continued, 'All I could do was try to make her last weeks as comfortable as possible. I scrubbed out the kitchen, which was our only heated room, and moved her bed into it. Put the kitchen cabinet in the living room, and moved the couch into the kitchen so I could be with her at night too. Each morning I talked to her about what meals she would like that day; then I shopped and cooked for the three of us.'

'The third being your little sister Paula?'

'That's right. My little stupid sister. I did all I could, but it's nothing in the face of death.' Tears trickled down my cheeks. They were real tears. When I'd recovered I said, 'She was given Extreme Unction, and died five days before Christmas—begging me with her last breath to try to make Christmas a peaceful time for the sake of Paula.'

'Excuse me,' he said; 'you told me she died on Christmas Eve.'

'Did I? I'm sorry; that was a mistake. She was buried on the twenty-third. I must have said that because Christmas Eve was when her death really hit me. I'd been invited to my married sister Geli's, and also by my friend Gustl's mother; but I couldn't bear to go anywhere. I stayed alone in the house. With the glowing Christmas tree... *Shit!'*

After a long silence he said, in a gentle voice, 'It's time; but stay here awhile if you want, to compose yourself. Then have your supper.'

6

There were tears of laughter in Gustl's eyes when I mentioned 'Herr Hakenkreuz'—a name I'd conjured up in the course of telling Dr Freud our concocted dream. 'Wonderful!' he roared. 'Adi, you're a genius!... Herr Hakenkreuz! On the river bank!' And we both rolled around on our chairs again in helpless mirth. 'You're playing him as an angler plays a fish, Adi!'

'Of course! And I'm sure he's going to make something of my mistake—and it was a pure mistake—of the date when mama died. I shall enjoy it.'

'Still no sign of Sophie.'

'No,' I sighed. 'Only her confounded sister. Who of course couldn't believe it when I appeared in my new... apparition...disguise! But I made one bad mistake, from the point of view of ever getting Sophie. Dr Freud came into the kitchen while I was scoffing chicken soup and being gazed at adoringly by Anna; he clapped me on the shoulder and said to her, "What do you think of our dandified young Jew?" I blurted out, "I'm not Jewish: whatever gave you the impression I was?" And they were both overcome with confusion. So I've torn it; but I could hardly tell a lie.'

'But they're thoroughly assimilated,' Gustl said. 'Maybe they'd *like* their daughter to marry an Aryan.'

'If I could even get to *see* her... And I must find some way of becoming Jewish again.'

He went back to doodling on the piano. 'I might have to kidnap her,' I said. During my desperate state in Linz, at the end of my tether with desire for Klara, I had meditated a mad plan to kidnap her. I would take her to some quiet hideaway in the country; she would love me and we would die together. I was often thinking of Crown Prince Rudolf, who in the year of my birth, 1889, had caused huge grief and scandal by dying in a double suicide with his young mistress, Mary Vetsera.

Father had told me part of the the story first, when I was about twelve. When he was not drunk, he could talk sensibly about politics, and was surprisingly progressive for such a stern patriarch. (I never, for instance, heard any anti-Semitic talk in our house.) Prince Rudolf, he told me, had been handsome and enlightened, the one great hope of the moribund Empire. Had he lived, papa said, he might have cleansed the Augean stable. He related the tragedy of his suicide with a mournful face, and did not mention the mistress. I had to wait a few years before I learned the whole story, including facts never publicly revealed. It appealed to my romantic temperament, and I dreamed of a similar fate with Klara.

The Crown Prince and his seventeen year old mistress had gone, in the depths of winter, to the imperial hunting lodge at Mayerling. The next morning, servants found both of them dead, lying on their bed in the lodge. The Prince, perhaps, despaired because of a cold unfulfilling marriage, or that his progressive ideas were not readily accepted by the stiff, conservative Emperor. That much, everyone knows. Mary had a small rose in one hand, given her by the Prince no doubt, a tear-stained handkerchief in the other. Her head stained with dried blood, the Prince's more badly mutilated, and his finger still crooked from the revolver-shots which had killed them both. Rudolf was taken off to lie in state, his death bringing universal grief; Mary was carried off to a lumber room while they decided what to do with her.

Scandal had to be avoided. She was washed, and then fully dressed, even to outdoor clothes: coat, shoes, veil, boa. Snow and ice covered the world in silence. Two of her uncles, black-coated, stern-faced, then walked out on each side of her, holding her up as if alive, taking her as far as the lodge gates, where a carriage awaited. Her rigid corset would have helped in maintaining her upright stance. Her uncles assisted her to enter the carriage, and she sat between them during a perilous, slithering journey to the village cemetery, where she was huddled into a hastily-dug grave in the hard earth. I have heard her furtive burial compared to that of Ophelia's in Shakespeare's *Hamlet*, and the resemblance had struck me too in my recent reading of the play.

Oh yes, I dreamed of finding such a romantic love-death with Klara. And now briefly, not very seriously, as Gustl thumped out the beginning of Beethoven's *Hammerklavier* sonata, I diverted myself with thoughts of somehow arranging to die with Sophie. She would write a letter to her papa and mama—as Mary Vetsera apparently did to her mother—saying she was happier to die with me than live without me.

Hanging in Dr Freud's waiting room was an engraving which showed a horrible succubus—incubus?—I'm not sure of the word, but male monster anyway, with leering eyes and mouth and a hooked nose, about to ravish a beautiful girl lying on her bed, naked except for a transparent garment. It brought back to me that legend about my grandmother. Tonight I decided to make a scene about it. Shaking off Dr Freud's offered handshake, I shrieked out, 'That engraving next-door is eating away at me! I hate it! I can't understand why you give it house room!'

The doctor, startled: 'Which engraving is that?'

'The one with that pure, lovely girl being squatted on by a—by a monster!'

'Fuseli's "Nightmare"... It *is* powerful, isn't it?'

'It's disgusting!'

'Why do you find it disgusting? It portrays a nightmare.'

'Because it's grossly anti-Semitic.'

About to sit down on his pharaonic throne, he paused, as if frozen, before gradually lowering himself. 'Anti-Semitic? I don't understand.'

I marched around the sofa, gesticulating. 'The monster is a Jew—the false stereotype of a Jew: surely you can see that?'

'I hadn't,' he said. 'Now please sit down, if you won't lie.'

I sat, still scowling. 'Look at it again. The short, squat figure, round face with bulging eyes, bulbous nose and thick slavering mouth! You can see the same depiction every week in the anti-Semitic press. He's a Jew—and getting ready to ravish that sweet Aryan girl... Then, no doubt, to whip her off into slavery. Such a vicious lie! Yet you, a Jewish father, display it in your waiting room!'

'I shall look at it again, as soon as we've finished.' He looked perturbed. Here was this young man, who had resembled a Jew, but now looked emphatically German-Austrian—and proclaimed himself to be that—hysterically upset by an 'anti-Semitic' engraving!

I said I found anti-Semitism hard to understand. Jewish art dealers, here in the Leopoldstadt, dealt with me more honestly than those of other races. I much preferred Jews to the Czechs and Poles. With my friend Gustl I'd been invited to attend musical evenings at cultured, rich

Jewish homes, and was impressed by a feeling there of pure German enlightenment. And so on.

'Good, good...' He couldn't get his cigar to light, shook it angrily, and seemed quite disconcerted. At last he pulled himself together, lit his cursed cigar, and said, 'I'd like to return to your mother, Wolf. She was your father's niece.'

'More or less. It's slightly more complicated than that. Cousins, really; but of course with the age difference she called him uncle.'

'I've noticed that you quite often move your hands as if to cover your genitals. I wonder why you do that?'

Ah, he's trying to disconcert *me!*—'I didn't know I was doing it. It's a natural place to lay one's hands, surely?'

'That's true... I have been thinking about your riverbank dream, and how—in reality—your mother was *not* with your little brother— Edmund, I believe his name was—when he was buried. That was an awful betrayal, wasn't it? Neither your father nor your mother could be bothered to go to his funeral!'

'It seems that way.'

'What on earth could they have been doing that was so important? More important than their child's funeral? Perhaps they were expecting a carpenter to call to mend a broken window frame!' A sarcastic little smile played over his lips. I was curious about what would come next. '—Or perhaps your father suspected Edmund was not his offspring, and physically stopped your mother from attending.'

Ah, so that's it! 'That's disgusting and insulting!'

'I'm sorry if I've upset you. It's just that any other suggestion seems equally nonsensical... Whatever the reason, it must have made you wonder if she could be trusted to attend your funeral, should you die. That even mother-love was not entirely trustworthy... And therefore you should consider landing on the bank where Mr Hakenkreuz stood... the Aryan fire-symbol...' I said nothing, waiting, gazing up at a picture of a Sphinx. I was amused at how he believed he was toying with me, as a cat toys with a mouse between its paws.

He broke the silence: 'Your mother was a glutton for punishment, Wolf! Thrown out by two jealous wives... but it didn't stop her coming back...'

'No. She was loyal to papa.'

'Your father obviously felt he could rely on her.'

'That's true. She was so good-hearted and hard-working.'

'And perhaps there was a little sexual compulsion too—on both sides.'

Ah, sex had to come into it! I scowled. 'Not on mama's side. She was pure, a good Catholic.'

'Ah, yes, I'm sorry; she was a good Catholic. When you look at the reclining girl in the engraving, which upset you so much, do you see your mother in her?'

'Partly. I also see the sweet, pure girl I loved hopelessly in Linz— Klara. The same name as my mother's.' He invited me to talk about her, and I did so: and the emotional distance I now felt from her diminished as I described her loveliness, and my passion for her. I said I couldn't bear to think of her being raped by such a bestial figure—and life was full of such beasts. 'She was so sweet. I was *sure* I'd win that lottery!... When I followed mama's coffin to the grave, I saw I was passing Klara's house. And she was there, in an upstairs window, gazing down at me with a sad, pitying smile. But women are weak! I heard she's married to some peacock of an officer. Women are weak, they are weak.'

'Your mother wasn't weak, Wolf. She endured several infant deaths, and the intense pain of her illness, stoically.'

'No, mama was strong.' I described how she'd endured as Dr Bloch pressed iodine-soaked gauze into her open, suppurating wound. I had genuine tears in my eyes.

'Do you blame the doctor for causing her that suffering?'

'No, no; Dr Bloch was just trying his best. He's a good man. And besides, he loved—' I stopped before I could say 'doing all he could for his patients' as my stomach was griped at that moment and I doubled over.

'He loved?'

The pain eased. 'He loved doing all he could for his patients.'

I could sense him gathering himself to strike, like a cobra. In angry tones he said, 'Well, so do I. At least I love doing my best for my patients when I feel they are cooperating by telling me the truth.' He leaned forward with an intense stare at me. A minute, two minutes, went by; a long ash gathered on his cigar, and dropped. He pulled himself upright, snapped his notebook shut, and said, 'This is a waste of my time! You are not being honest.'

I leapt to my feet, walked around, shook my fists, and poured out a loud stream of abuse.

'Sit down!' he shouted. 'This is intolerable!'

I sat down, muttering an apology. Then said, 'I am always honest with you!'

'Rubbish! Dr Bloch is alive, you said he *is*—not was—a good man; you would have continued by saying he *loves* doing his best for his patients, if that was what you intended to say. He loved your mother— is that it? Come! Answer me! There's no point if you're going to lie, Wolf.'

Ah! How absurd! This fellow had his own form of violence. I hung my head as I whispered, 'Yes. I believe so.'

A gentler voice now: 'Did your mother love him?'

Mama forgive me, but I was caught up in the drama of the moment. Besides, she'd have been better off loving Dr Bloch than my brute of a father.

'Yes.'

'They had an affair?'

I let my imagination roam, as Gustl does when improvising on the keys. 'It could hardly be called that, it was so brief. They—went to bed together two or three times, in as many weeks, then both of them drew back, horrified. Mama revealed it in her last confession to her priest, and afterwards repeated it to me, with tears in her eyes.'

'Tell me. Tell me what she said had happened.'

'She said it was a momentary weakness, and all mixed up with her first three babies falling ill and dying, one after the other. Dr Bloch was very attentive and compassionate, as he always is. It didn't matter to him whether you were Jew or Gentile, rich or poor. She was sobbing one day, she said, and he put his arms around her to comfort her.'

'Ah, that was kind of him!' The sarcastic little smile. Momentarily he glanced aside and up at a large photograph of a bosomy tight-laced young woman swooning back into the arms of a handsome man, not unlike a younger Freud.

'Yes,' I agreed, 'but of course it wasn't just kindness; she was *so* sweet and lovely and must have been even more so then, in her mid-twenties. I wish I had known her then! And the doctor is an attractive, cultured man. It seemed he had very little comfort of that sort at home. So they both, briefly, weakened. She was so ashamed.'

I saw his face soften; even grow tender. 'Grief,' he said gently, 'often walks hand in hand with desire. It's the assertion of life against death. I felt it myself when my father died. *Sunt lachrymae rerum...*'

'Is that Latin?' When he nodded I said with some real bitterness, 'I was never taught it; they didn't think we were good enough at our technical school.'

'I'm sorry. It means the tears of things.'

'It was such a little while that they were lovers. Just two or three weeks. A temporary madness; then she pulled back.'

'Well, well... These things can happen... And I can't believe it was a shallow fling. I'm sure Dr Bloch would have loved her in a serious way, suffering all the torments of a Jewish conscience. You didn't say he *had* loved her, but that he still loved her. Right to the end, h'mm?'

I decided to jerk myself around on the sofa, until I was almost lying stretched out on it. I mumbled, "I have no idea; how could I tell? He was always a kind doctor. I told you, with the iodine treatment, he was cruel to be kind; he hoped it would work.'

'I'm sure he did... But so like love, h'mm?—first the tenderness, then the agonising pain... It was awful for you too, young man. Your mental torture was as great as hers. Your precious, beautiful mama, dying too young, in such agony.' Gentle tones, as if he were stroking his victim's brow. A tear trickled down my cheek—simply from remembering my mother's agony.

'I know it's painful to remember,' he went on, in the same gentle voice. 'But I'd like to know about Christmas Eve, the day after the funeral. You stayed alone in your house, refusing all invitations. Just you and the glowing Christmas tree.'

Almost inaudibly: 'Yes.' This too was painful indeed; I had no need to act as if on stage.

'Your little sister presumably was with your half-sister—Geli?— and her husband?' I nodded my head. 'How terrible for you! Such memories! Of happiness—of pain... Picturing her brightness and health, at happier Christmases. One of those days that later one doesn't know how one endured them.' Another nod from me, another trickling tear. 'How did you manage to get through the day? Do you remember what you did?'

I pulled himself to my feet, took a pace or two from the couch, waving my arms; I said in a strangled voice, 'Could we leave this?'

'Please sit down.' I glanced towards the door as if contemplating a bolt for safety, then sat. 'I do know it's painful. We have to get at these painful things. What did you do?'

'I took some flowers to the grave. Otherwise I don't remember a single thing.'

'Perhaps you took farewell of your mother by looking at mementoes: clothes, photographs, little personal items; that sort of thing.'

'I think I did look around. In a daze.'

He nodded. 'That would be the natural thing to do. Hunting for documents too, because death leaves a lot of loose ends.'

'I may have done that.'

'Of course you did. You were the loving and dutiful son, the man of the house. You found little trinkets and cards that brought your mother poignantly to life—and yet she was in the cold grave... Your mother died properly for you that day. That's what you told us—"she died on Christmas Eve".' He gave a jump in his chair and leaned forward, and his voice was harsher: 'What made you feel that day was her real death for you? H'mm? Well, in giving me two versions of the day when she died you may just have made a slip of the tongue; though it's not something one would easily forget. Did you see no one at all that Christmas Eve?'

I brushed the tears from my eyes. 'No one. I did think the father might come to see me; full of pious platitudes about love and redemption and eternal life and so on. But he didn't.'

Urgently he leaned forward. 'Your father? You thought he might come? But he was dead!'

'I didn't say *my* father. *The* father—our priest. Mama often called him that, "the father".'

'Oh, but you did say "my father"! You meant Dr Bloch. He was your real father, wasn't he? Come now, you probably found a love letter, while rifling through a bedroom cabinet; and the date on it probably told you the affair hadn't been so short after all!'

This was quite unbelievable! I hunched forward, my head in my hands, and gave a groan of anguish. 'A love letter, yes. Not from that lecherous swine Bloch—from my mother to him; unfinished, never sent; dated 1891, two years after I was born. Intimate, yearning, scented with roses. She almost wished, she wrote, one of the family would fall sick— not too badly—so he would visit and... It was clear they were still—'

'Lovers.'

Poor dear mama, forgive me. You couldn't even write. You signed with a cross. Forgive my lie. I hadn't had to scheme, he was setting the trap to catch himself in! 'Yes! He corrupted her, that Jewish swine! How do you know so much—ferryman?'

'By observing my fellow man closely, Wolf. Nothing more. Don't be too hard on your mother. And it doesn't necessarily mean you're Jewish, my friend. You could just as easily be the Customs officer's son.'

I pretended to pause, as if it was painful to go on, sighing, twisting around—but really to give myself time to invent. 'That isn't so. Mama wrote that her one consolation was her little Wolf, and how grateful she was there was no possible doubt that he—that I was—his son. She thanked God that "Uncle" had not bothered her at all, that spring when I was conceived, coming home too drunk to care. But now—well, "uncle" was bothering her, and this added to her despair... Oh, it was quite a letter, Dr Freud!'

'So she died to you when you read it.'

What do words matter? By lying I was preserving my true memory of her in my own private sanctuary. I said, 'Her purity was smirched, yes. I looked out through the window and saw a line of horse droppings in the snow. That's how I felt about her. Though of course I still pitied and loved her.'

'Of course.' Then, harshly: 'But why have you been wasting my time? Why didn't you tell me this at the very start?'

'I—I'm sorry, I—'

'Oh well, it can't be helped. It's time. Go and have your supper.'

And to my joy, Sophie visited the kitchen while I was being served by the maid. She pretended to be fetching some cheese; but there was no mistaking the blush that came into her cheeks. She sat and talked for a few minutes: her eyes so gay and sparkling and gazing into mine. The sparkle scarcely dimmed when she told me Anna was in bed, not very well. I asked her to pass on my good wishes for a speedy recovery. I also confessed that I was feeling a degree of shock—though not an unpleasant one—in that her brilliant father had compelled me to accept I was Jewish. And that this was something to be proud of. I wished for nothing more than to live in a close, loving Jewish family home, as hers so evidently was.

I wished to say so much more, and I felt that she did too; but there was no chance to, with the cursed ugly maid hovering. However, as she was showing me out, Sophie thrilled me to ecstasy by saying, 'Papa is to give a lecture at the University on Tuesday evening, at eight, on the psychology of a famous Italian artist—I forget his name. He's been writing a case study of him. I think he would be honoured if you felt like attending.' She squeezed my arm. 'It's open to the public, and as an artist... well, I thought you might be interested.' Those incredible, wide, demure yet seductive eyes!

I stammered that the honour would be all mine. I walked away from the house not conscious of my footsteps.

7

And so it was that I found myself sitting near the back of a crowded lecture hall, listening to Dr Freud expatiate on the psychology of a Florentine sculptor, Donatello, dead these five hundred years. The gist of his talk—and I always try to find the gist—was that Donatello was a homosexual in love with his mother. He used, as backdrop, giant reproductions of the famous slender bronze *David* in the Bargello Museum and his wooden (I speak of the material , not in terms of its emotional power) Magdalene. His thesis was that David was a self-portrait, idealised, slender, beautiful, erotic, *as seen by his mother*. He argued, insofar as I could follow the drift, that Donatello's mother had adored him so completely that the adult artist could love no one else; but he constantly searched for a male lover whom he could love as overwhelmingly as his mother had loved him. His tragic, ravaged Magdalene, entirely stripped of her early erotic self, was his acknowledgement in old age that his hopes had been vain. No one could match up to the love of one's mother. He confessed that much of his theory was speculation, as we knew little about Donatello's life.

During questions, Anna, in the front row far beneath me, asked a question about homo-erotic love that I thought far beyond her years, but her father answered it patiently if fairly incomprehensibly. Sophie, to my dismay, was not present. After Anna's question a bunch of half-a-dozen rowdies marched down the aisle shouting that Dr Freud was a disgrace to Vienna with his perverted ideas. A few people cheered, many more booed or howled them down. I tended to agree with the protesters, but if Sophie had been present I might have found the courage to stand up and denounce them as attempting to deny free speech. However, since she was not there, it would have been a complete waste of time and effort and I stayed in my seat.

I walked home in a surly mood. Almost more than Sophie's absence what disturbed me was that this so-called intellectual had the insolence to pretend to examine the soul of a fellow artist—one of much greater genius than I, but a fellow artist nonetheless—who had gone down to his ancestors so many centuries ago.

When I arrived for my next appointment the maid met me at the door and thrust a thick envelope into my hand, saying curtly, 'Dr Freud can't see you this evening. He asked me to give you this.'

My face burning, I rushed down the marble stairs, up the hill, and sat down in a street-corner coffee shop. I tore open the envelope. Several bank-notes fell out. I devoured the letter, a long one, written in an elegant script...

'Dear Wolf,

I am sorry that I cannot see you this evening, or indeed in the future. There are two reasons for my decision. First, I am troubled by your manner. I am used to deception from clients; they lie to me regularly, but always to defend their deepest feelings, which they themselves do not recognise. They lie, but with pain. You, however, strike me as deceiving me, lying with a positive glee. Your aggressive movements and gestures also disturb me.

Secondly, and much the more importantly: we are too much alike. That seems an extraordinary statement, since our conditions in life are so different; but it's true. My father too was elderly when I first knew him; and my mother was young, beautiful, pure. My children would be amazed by this, since now she strikes them merely as an old, peevish lady, screeching at them in Yiddish. But she was, when I first set eyes on her, beautiful and enchanting, and she loved me totally.

My father, like yours—your *nominal* father, that is—had had two earlier wives, one of them quite mysterious. And I had, like you, older—much older—half-brothers who 'disappeared'; in their case to England. I had also, like you, a younger brother who died. I had been unconsciously, innocently, jealous of him.

And then, there are our always mysterious origins. Aged three, you were moved by your parents from Braunau am Inn to, ultimately, Linz. I was moved from a small Moravian town, at three years old, to Vienna. Strangely, I still have a yearning for Freiberg, my 'Eden' in Moravia—just as yours is, I think, the bleak and primitive Waldviertel. We all carry our Eden around with us. Though I can have no conscious memory of Freiberg, I still feel that I am from that air, from that soil.

And behind that, it now appears, we both have some unknowable Galician *shtetl*, in that unimaginable Sheol of our persecuted past.

It is too much! We have too much likeness. When we are together I think too much of myself, and it gets in the way of objective therapy.

I hope I have been able to help you a little. I wish you well. I think you are extremely talented. I am haunted by your dream of the river crossing. While I am sure I am an incompetent ferryman, I'm also sure that the choice lies in your hands. I feel you could land on either bank—but the choice of which, the light or the dark, is up to you. I was particularly struck by your revolutionary ideas for housing, and I believe, with application, you could one day become an excellent city planner or architect. You must work hard! The enclosed small sum may not be enough to pay for training, but should at least pay for a few steak dinners to build up your strength!

Please forgive my desertion. I have agonised over it.

> Yours very sincerely,
> Sigmund Freud'

I was still reading the last sentences, seething with anger and humiliation, when I heard a familiar voice, unfamiliarly agitated. 'Wolf, thank God I've found you!' Anna. She was breathing heavily as if she had been running; her face white, her eyes stary, her hair wild. She undid the belt of her long black coat, and slipped into the seat beside me. 'I saw you leave, from my window; I hoped you were coming in here rather than racing off further.'

'I was sent packing by your fucking father!' I said angrily. I did not regret the coarse expletive, nor did Anna flinch at it. She placed her hand over mine on the table. 'I know. I'm so sorry.'

'Didn't even have the courage to tell me to my face, but had your maid thrust a letter at me!'

She glanced down at the scattered pages and the notes. 'I know; father told me. I'm really sorry.' She looked miserable and ill, and I thought she had probably been crying. It gave to her rather plain, though intelligent, face a kind of wistful appeal, and my feelings softened towards her. 'It's not your fault,' I said, as I stowed the letter and notes in my pocket. A waiter came up and she ordered two cups of coffee, adding to me that it was her turn to pay.

And you've not had anything to eat, Wolf,' she said; 'would you like a cake?'

I was hungry, and I have a sweet tooth. I let her ask for the dessert trolley to be wheeled up and I chose a chocolate cake. She pressed me to take something else and I took a marzipan slice. Our coffee came. Biting into the delicious marzipan, I said, 'He accuses me of lying to him; and says we're too alike. That's shit!'

'I know. But it's not the real reason. Or at least not the main one. It's true he felt, wrongly I'm sure, that you enjoyed evading the truth at times; and it's true that he's been moved and even disturbed by resemblances in your family situation. But...' She plucked a handkerchief from her pocket and rubbed her eyes; sighed and looked troubled. 'But it's mainly something else. I don't quite know how to tell you.'

The chocolate cake was equally delicious. I dabbed crumbs from my mouth. 'Go on, please,' I said; 'I can hardly be more hurt than I have been already.'

Large expressive brown eyes gazed into mine. 'They think—mama and papa think—that my interest in you is too intense and too personal. It's ridiculous of course; I do care for you, care a lot, but it's only because I think you have a fine character but don't have much luck in your life. It's friendship—you know that.'

'Yes, and I've been very grateful for it.'

A drum beat faintly from a street not far off, and voices—probably Serbian, I thought—began chanting slogans. Another street demonstration. Just as when I had coffee with Anna and Sophie, delicious as marzipan, after the Karl May lecture. I would probably never see her again. A pang of anguish.

'I've not been terribly well lately,' Anna continued. 'Migraine, stomach cramps. It's just because the exams were stressful, and I'm sure I'll soon feel better now I'm on holiday. School is over, forever. At least as a schoolgirl; I'm going to be training to teach.'

'Well, that's nice; you'll make an excellent teacher. Just as your father thinks I'd make an excellent town planner!'

'Anyway, it will be months before I start that. I'm free. I'll take long walks in the fresh air and soon feel well. But they think my sickness has been caused by my mooning over *you!* A lovesick schoolgirl! It's quite absurd.' Her wistful, mooning eyes made me uncomfortable and I looked away. Her voice hurried on: 'I think Sophie has planted that idea in their heads. She can't *bear* me to feel happy. And she's papa's favourite, so he would believe anything she said. He calls her his "Sunday child", simply because she doesn't have a serious thought in her head but is always singing and laughing.'

I imagined her sweet voice. I would never get to hear her sing. Sadness swept over me, followed by a renewal of rage against the insufferable letter. What a way to treat me! But entirely typical of my life. When I'd applied for Art College, they too couldn't look behind my poverty and my lack of proper schooling to see my burning talent, and turned me down.

'Your father gave me conscience money,' I said, feeling in my pocket. 'Let me pay for this.'

'No, no, I entreat you.'

'Well, thank you, Anna. Now I must get back to my dismal, airless room and my piano-thumping friend.' I stood up. 'It's been very nice knowing you.' I held out my hand. She looked miserable, ignored the offered hand-shake.

'It mustn't end like this. Please sit down, Wolf, I have more to say. Have another dessert.' She signalled to our waiter. Then took my hand and pulled me firmly back down in my chair.

She waited while I selected another cake from the trolley, then said —a blush rising into her wan cheeks—'I could take over from my father, Wolf. I know I would seem amateurish compared to my brilliant father'

'—Oh, he didn't get anywhere with me.'

'Then it's possible I would. Papa talks to me a lot about his cases, and I've read all his books. I'm passionately interested in the new psychology. In fact I would like to make that a career, only papa probably thinks I don't have the intelligence for it. But if I could prove to him that I'm capable, by helping you a little…'

I felt sorry for her. The flame of longing danced over her cheeks. While I ate my orange-flavoured cake she stammered out that I would be doing her a great favour, giving her experience; I would have to be very tolerant of her mistakes, which would be legion; that of course we couldn't meet at the apartment, but was my friend, my pianist friend, *always* present in my room? She could visit me there.

I could scarcely believe this young girl was making such a suggestion; yet I knew she had no idea how I or others might see it as indecent. She was pure; she wasn't a female of the 'Schnitzler' kind. Her innocence and her desperation—to go on meeting me—made me feel generous.

'It's true, Gustl isn't there most days,' I said; 'he's at the Conservatorium. And Frau Guttman, our nosy landlady, visits her aged mother on Mondays and Fridays…'

Her eyes were shining with joy, she laid her hand over mine. 'Then you'll say yes?'

I reflected, wiping the last of the cake from my lips. It would be a tenuous link still with Sophie. I might sometimes persuade Anna to bring her sister, to a concert or opera, say.

'It would need to be more of a dialogue. I would need to feel I could ask you questions too, about your parents, your sister, and so on.'

'Anything you say… Of course it would have to be a complete secret. If papa knew I was still seeing you, he would be utterly furious, he would never forgive me.'

That settled it for me. It would be such sweet revenge. I asked her how it could be a complete secret if she hoped to use it as a way of showing him that she had a potential for success in this field. She stammered and flushed and could not find an answer. She was really saying, Look, I want to see you again, I couldn't bear to say goodbye; and she looked content that I knew this was her real motive.

We arranged to meet in a few days, at my lodgings. I wrote the address and drew a map on a napkin. She said, 'Thank you, thank you a thousand times' as we shook hands on parting.

On my way home I came upon the noisy demonstration. Serb Nationalists indeed, and they were being abused and set upon by German Nationalists. Skirting the edge of it, I got in one strong blow to a Serbian kidney, then flitted away.

8

'Fräulein, how nice to see you again!'

Her hand flew to her throat. I had startled her, stepping out of the shadows. 'Oh yes, how nice!'

'I wondered if you would do me the honour of drinking a coffee with me?'

'Oh!... I would love to, only I am rushing to meet mama. She's helping me to pick out some... some clothes. I'm sorry. Another time perhaps.'

And with that Sophie hurried on, but blessing me with that radiant smile. I felt she had spoken sincerely and I was not too downcast.

Later that day Gustl and I had an encounter with a much older and much more characteristic Viennese female. The woman in question had advertised a room in a reasonably pleasant part of the city, at not too exorbitant a rent. When we found the house it looked promising from the outside. A servant ushered us in and led us to a drawing room. We sat perched on easy chairs and waited. At last the lady of the house swept in, wearing little, it appeared, under a white negligee. I guessed she was fifty, plump, with a florid face grotesquely over-painted, and with a mop of obviously dyed blond hair. She greeted us effusively, apologised for her undress as she had been having a siesta, and sat down opposite us. The room began to reek of some atrocious perfume. She chatted to us in an affected voice about our lives, fluttering long eyelashes. She was recently widowed, she said, and needed to augment her pension. Her negligee increasingly parted, exposing panties and nipples.

I jumped to my feet, said she was very kind but really the rent would overstretch our budget. She said, crestfallen, 'Let me at least show you the room; it's possible I could lower the rent for two such well-spoken and charming young men,' but I was already half out the door, Gustl hurrying red-faced in my wake.

Out in the street I exclaimed, 'Ouf! What an awful woman! She was clearly intent on seducing us both, Gustl. God knows what disease she'd have given us!'

He shrugged. 'I suppose you're right.'

I know I am. She's a whore.'

He revealed his innocence by saying, 'I thought she seemed quite pleasant.'

I told him to scrub his hands when we got home, for she had shaken our hands and one didn't know where hers had last been.

It was easy to see that Anna, privileged daughter of of a well-to-do family, had never before set foot in such a slum building as ours, nor entered such a seedy and cluttered room as Gustl and I shared. I could see her flinch as I opened the door to her timid knock and stepped back for her to come in. She merely said how nice it was that we had a piano. She took off her hat and gloves, looked around for a hanger or clothes hook, could not see any, so laid her expensive garments on the unmade bed.

I shouldn't put them there,' I said; 'unless you want to go home itching from fleas and lice.' She grimaced, and snatched the garments up. 'Just put them on that chair,' I said. 'You take the other one and I'll sit on the bed.'

'Really you should lie down, Wolf.'

'I didn't with your father.'

'Well, alright then; whatever makes you feel more comfortable.' She sat awkwardly on the simple, wooden chair, which rocked slightly on one leg, and nervously smoothed her plain dirndl skirt down over her knees and almost to her ankles. 'Well, where shall we start?' she asked. 'I'm really terrified, Wolf. You can probably hear my stomach growling.'

'I thought it was mine.'

'No, it's mine.'

'My stomach is always growling.'

'Like a real wolf!' She smiled. Quite a joyful smile. Joyful, it was easy to interpret, because she was here with me. 'Papa admitted to me that because you refused to lie down *he* found himself talking too much, instead of allowing you to bring up anything that was in your head. But —I remember what you said about sharing things between us, so that it's more equal, and I'm happy with that.'

'Good. That's the way I want it.'

'This is really a very odd situation. You will have to be merciful to me. We'll think of it as just chatting, at least at first. You look—distant, faraway. Tell me what you're thinking about?'

I put on what I hoped was a genial expression. 'If you must know, I was thinking that it's strange your parents wish you to teach—to have a career. Really you should be with your mother learning how to cook, clean, sew and knit better, for your role in life.'

She stiffened. 'Oh, and what's that?'

'To be a good, efficient wife and mother, of course. *Kinder, Küche, Kirche*. Well, not *Kirche* in your case, of course.'

'I think your views are rather old-fashioned.'

I responded with a shrug.

'As a matter of fact, I can knit very well! Better than my mother. I knit a lot; I enjoy it; it's very relaxing.' She fell silent, looking thoughtful, then continued: 'I don't expect to get married. I'm not pretty like my sister. And sooner or later my parents will expect me to look after them.' With some bitterness: 'That's the role allotted to the youngest daughter.'

'So you are jealous of Sophie?'

'Oh no, not really! She doesn't have an idea in her pretty little head! You hardly ever see her reading. Only she laughs and jokes and sings a lot, and I suppose that charms papa, whose life has to be very serious. And mother doesn't give him much joy. What do you think of marriage, Wolf?' Without giving me a chance to reply she hurried on: 'I'm not sure what to think of it. From those I've observed, boredom sets in after a few years. Perhaps the only alternative to boredom is hatred! My parents don't hate each other, that's clear; but they have little to say to each other. Mama takes care of the running of the household; papa has his absorbing work, in which she takes no interest whatever; so they have less to talk about than a couple of business partners would have. But they're stuck together, almost like Siamese twins joined at the head. Papa has much more in common with Minna, mama's spinster sister who lives with us. He's more cheerful and convivial when she is around; and quite often they go on walking holidays together. If my father were not so incorrigibly upright, one might suspect they did more than walk. I should not entirely blame him: Aunt Minna is lively and intelligent, whereas mama is—a pretty dull *Hausfrau*.'

'"*Incorrigibly* upright" is a rather strange expression.'

She flushed. 'You're right. I meant impeccably upright.' She looked miserable. 'I'm doing this all wrong. I'm hopeless at it.'

I didn't want her deciding to give up; she was my lifeline to Sophie. 'No, no!' I assured her. 'I actually feel more comfortable than with your father. We are both young, so I can relate to you better.' Her face brightened. I decided to feed her a morsel of truth. 'I had a nightmare last night, from which I awoke screaming. I was buried alive, could hardly breathe. I hammered at the coffin lid, and tried to shout, but my voice was too weak. There was another body lying next to me, in the same coffin. Snow was falling—I could see it above ground, and two grief-stricken men standing there in long black coats, deaf to my shouts. I'm pretty sure I was thinking of Mary Vetsera and Crown Prince Rudolf. You of course know that tragic event, twenty three years ago?'

Naturally she knew of the Crown Prince's suicide, she said, but she had not heard of Mary Vetsera. She only knew that Rudolf had died because of extreme melancholia. Wasn't his mother, the Empress Elisabeth, mad? And then stabbed to death in Paris: a madwoman murdered by a madman...

'Ah, so you don't know about Prince Rudolf's mistress! Their fate moves me tremendously. Let me describe for you a wintry morning at Mayerling, the imperial hunting lodge, in coincidentally the year of my birth, '89... Two black-coated, stern-faced middle-aged men and their seventeen-year-old niece, Mary Vetsera, walk out of the lodge. Nothing very unusual, you may say, in two uncles walking out with their pretty niece between them—except that this niece, Mary, is dead! I'm not surprised you don't know this part of the story; it was hushed up. Rudolf and Mary were desperately in love. They must have realised their future was hopeless. So they travelled to Mayerling and...' I described, colourfully and almost rhapsodically, their night together, in chaste terms suitable for a girl; the gift of the rose; the two shots ringing out, alarming the servants who came rushing. The summoning of Mary's uncles, the dressing of Mary, limp in the hands of the weeping servant-girls; then her uncles clasping her firmly between them and walking out; her feet dragging but hidden by her long skirt; her corset, even more severe in those days, helping to support her; the shameful secret burial in a village churchyard...

Anna's eyes were huge, gazing at me; her lips were parted in wonderment. I gave, I may say, a passionate, almost mesmeric, performance. It's so easy to mesmerize girls. It was clear the bosomy, tight-laced girl swooning back into a man's arms on Freud's wall—a demonstration of treating 'hysteria', Anna had told me—was mesmerized by him. Anna's expression resembled hers. All she said at the end of my poetic speech was, 'That's amazing, Wolf.'

She forgot to talk about my nightmare. We were both silent. I watched a cockroach glide from under the bed and move swiftly before vanishing in a gap between floorboards.

I said, 'Actually, Anna, though I was too frightened at the time, when I look back at the day when you and your father grabbed my arms and propelled me along the streets to your home, I think how much the scene resembled that strange trio at Mayerling! I was little more than a corpse, blind and helpless... But now, it's time; Gustl will be back soon and I must do some drawings, otherwise I won't eat tomorrow.'

'Yes, yes, I must go.' She stood up in a daze; as if sleepwalking she moved to open the door, and I had to say to her, 'You're forgetting your hat and gloves!'

9

'That's how I shall die, one day, Anna, in a double death with a woman by my side. It's fated. A gypsy fortune-teller in the Prater told me that, among things which have already happened and which were uncannily true.' Of course the fortune-teller had said no such thing, but it seemed a pleasant embroidery.

Anna had started by saying she had thought of little else but the tragic love-story in the three days since our last meeting. After blurting out the fictitious prophecy I cursed myself for an idiot. If I should ever be in a position to pay court to the beautiful Sophie, it would hardly help to have a bitterly jealous sister tell her I foresaw dying together with my wife or mistress! But I needn't have worried—Anna immediately exclaimed that she would love to have her fortune told by that gypsy, and perhaps I could take her one day?

I shrugged a perhaps; then said, 'Actually she wasn't infallible; she said I was certainly not Jewish. I had always felt I probably was, despite my very Austrian-German, Roman Catholic home.' I added diplomatically, 'And I was happy to believe myself Jewish, though I also wished I wasn't so poor. But then your father—how much has he talked to you about our meetings?'

'Oh, nothing at all. You were his patient for that brief while, so he observed complete confidence.'

'Well, I told you we didn't get anywhere. That wasn't quite true. By a series of brilliant questions and deductions he compelled me to admit something I had buried deep in my—I think you call it the unconscious. That our family doctor, a Jew, had had an affair with my mother, and I was his son.'

She looked startled. 'Good heavens!... Well, you did look like a Jew from the east, until you...'

'Smartened up! Yes.'

'But how can you be sure you're the doctor's son?'

'I found a love letter from my mother to Dr Bloch, in which she said she knew I was his son, because my ostensible father had been too drunk to have marital relations with her around the time of my conception. She had presumably intended to hand it to him, under the pretext of some sickness, but then lost her nerve. But forgot to destroy it.' I related this sincerely, since I had almost come to believe it myself. The desolate house, the ironic Christmas tree lights, the suffering youth opening her bureau, finding the letter, his poor mother's hopeless yearning... How sad.

'Well, thank you for telling me. Not that it makes any difference— I mean, to how I see you. And actually it doesn't make you Jewish, strictly speaking.'

It was my turn to be startled. 'Why not?'

'Jewishness is passed through the maternal line.'

'That's ridiculous!... In any case, Jewish blood came in much earlier.' I adroitly changed the family legend to make my paternal grandmother Jewish.

'I hardly feel Jewish at all,' Anna said. And made that curious gesture of wiping her chest, as if wiping off a stain. 'Our home is purely German, as you've had a glimpse of. German culture. Though when we visit my grandmother, papa's mother, which we do every Sunday, then I see how recent the transformation has been. She's a vulgar, smelly, sniping, whining old lady, still reeking of the *shtetl* she came from! Talking Yiddish too. It's a strange meeting of different worlds, with papa speaking his pure, beautiful German. I don't really like going there. And yesterday was especially unpleasant.'

'Why was that?'

'Oh, Max was with us. He's visiting us at present. He's Sophie's fiancé from Hamburg.'

An ice-cold hand squeezed my heart. 'I didn't know she was engaged to be married.'

'Oh, haven't we mentioned it? Yes. I'm not jealous of her marrying Max. He's so stuffy and conventional, and his breath smells. And yesterday they were forever talking about her trousseau, and wedding dress, and so on... You would think she was the first girl ever to get married! That's if she *does* end up marrying him; it's months away and she's very flighty. But I do love her, I don't want you to get the wrong impression.'

'Oh I don't.' I could only think, with despair, that the girl I had begun to think of as *my* Sophie belonged to someone else. How foolish of me to imagine I could step into that world. One stroke of good luck, that was all I needed, but I wasn't meant to have it. Just grinding poverty and illness.

Vaguely I heard her speak, as if in counterpoint, about her being a very fortunate person, living in such a close, reasonably well-off family, and with such a brilliant and distinguished father. Who would sometimes dandle her still on his lap. Those were happy moments!

'Not like *my* sweet-natured father,' I snarled, angry and frustrated. 'Coming home drunk night after night, then getting the strap out and— *beat—twenty eight—beat—twenty nine—beat—thirty!*'—swinging my arm in imitation as I shouted the words. Though papa had rarely gone above twenty blows; he needed to save some for mama.

'Awful! Awful! Poor Wolf...' She seemed to shrink back on her chair, her hands clasped tight in her lap. The mimed blows affected her almost as powerfully as if she herself were receiving them. Her face was quivering. I was touched, despite my rage and disappointment, by her sympathy, the purity of her young untouched soul. And suddenly, in a way I had never experienced, her sweetness, purity and compassion for my childhood sufferings started to dissolve the ice around my heart. I felt calm again. Even my stomach ceased its constant mutterings. My mind withdrew to snowy mountain peaks, with green fields stretched below. What did it matter that Sophie was engaged? The marriage wasn't inevitable. Girls can change their minds. She was 'flighty', Anna had said.

I stood up from the bed, went to a small cupboard and took out my latest picture, a watercolour showing an Alpine scene. I showed it to Anna. She said, I thought with some surprise, 'Oh, that's beautiful, Wolf!'

'Thank you. I don't just do little sketches of buildings on postcards!'

'I can see that. What inspired you to paint this scene?' She returned it to me and I sat back down on the bed.

'I painted it yesterday, from sketches I made during an adventure I had last summer with Gustl. You must meet him sometime. It was a day I'll never forget. We took the train to Semmering; that wonderful journey, rising and curving constantly, all the tunnels and viaducts, up to a thousand metres. We got out at Semmering. Blue sky everywhere; above us the snowy peaks, below us the brilliant green meadows dotted with churches. It was quite magical, Anna! It conjured up for me all our wonderful Germanic legends. We had plenty of time till the last train back, so we walked and walked, in our threadbare clothes and our thin shoes with holes in them! Up and up, pausing only for me to make some sketches. We climbed a mountain peak, perhaps the Rax, but we weren't sure. We didn't care. Just the height and the splendid view were intoxicating!'

Her eyes were wide, and I could see she was entirely entranced by the scene I was conjuring up; or by me, or probably both. I went on: 'We hadn't noticed the weather changing. Suddenly the sky was black, and huge raindrops were falling. We stumbled back the way we had come, but got hopelessly lost. We were soaked and cold and hungry. We had just a crust of bread between us, which we shared and wolfed down. But somehow we didn't worry; it was all part of a great adventure, a joyous encounter with nature… And when it was almost dark, we spotted a hut. A shepherds' hut, I suppose, and we crawled inside. We stripped off our trousers and jackets, shivering as we tried to wring them dry. There was a pile of hay, and then Gustl found on a high shelf some squares of canvas. I think the peasants use them to carry hay down to the valley. He made me take off my shirt and underwear, and lie down on the hay, which luckily was dry, and then he tenderly rolled me up in canvas. Then he did the same for himself. And we were quite snug and warm all night… listening to the rain and the wind. And in the morning, the sun was out and our clothes almost dry. We soon got down to the train station. My God, we were so hungry though!…'

She went on smiling and nodding her head after I had finished. She said, 'The way you described it, it's almost like a mystical experience. Did you feel that?'

'When I'm out in nature with all its beauty, I do feel as if I'm a part of everything, and I'm aware of some higher presence. I'm not sure I believe in God, but one can't deny there's *something*.'

'Papa wouldn't agree with you; he's an atheist. I'm not sure he's right on that… And you obviously have a beautiful friendship, you and Gustl. I loved the way you said he "tenderly" rolled you in the canvas. Love between people of the same sex can be so… pure… What are you going to do with your picture? Are you hoping to sell it?'

'I shall try one of the dealers,' I said.

'How much would you ask for it? I'd love to buy it—that's if I could afford it.'

A moment of generosity: 'I'd like to give it to you as a present.'

'Oh no, I couldn't!'

'I insist; you're trying to help me. And I'm not destitute at the moment; I had a small money gift from an aunt, and I'm still eking out the money your father so generously gave me.'

'Well, I would have to hide it, of course.'

'Why? You could say you came upon me selling my pictures, liked this one, and gave me a small sum for it. You could show your father— well, and Sophie too—to prove I'm not entirely without artistic talent.'

'Yes, perhaps I could.' She was studying it minutely. 'It's signed A. Hitler,' she said. I explained that I sometimes had to change my name in order to keep ahead of the draft. She nodded, saying she quite understood and didn't blame me.

She went off, aglow, with my carefully rolled-up picture. Gustl, when he arrived back a short time after, was dismayed that I had given it away. I told him about Sophie's being engaged, and said this was my first counter-attack after retreat. Anna would rush to show the watercolour to her sister—who would be astonished by its quality, and contrast my creative talent with the stodginess of her fiancé. 'You're an artful devil, Adi!' Gustl said with a chuckle. 'Who else but you could break up an engagement with a watercolour given to the girl's sister! It's a masterstroke!'

'But my first thought was a kind one. Mama used to say that it's more blessed to give than to receive.'

'Your mother was a saint.'

10

It was the first time I had seen Anna angry. Icily angry. Colder than the unseasonably chill June day outside. She fobbed off my attempt to help her off with her coat. She sat, but kept her coat and gloves on, as if this would be a very short visit.

'What's the matter, Anna?'

'My father was right. You told him lies. You've told *me* lies. When there was no need to. Not just covering something painful up, but inventing. For no reason except to make fools of us.'

'I don't understand.'

'My father took me aside after supper last night and said, "Anna, that young man we tried to help—Stiedler—was a scoundrel, a patholo-gical liar." He explained that he's acquainted with this Dr Bloch from Linz; he comes occasionally to the B'rai B'rith, the Jewish discussion group in Vienna. And by chance papa met him at one of these a few evenings ago. He mentioned you; and Dr Bloch indeed remembered you well, though going by a different name—Hitler, I imagine—and said you'd been wonderfully attentive to your mother in her final weeks. So that is to your credit.'

She blushed slightly, and looked pleased momentarily, but then rushed on: 'Said your father was a stiff, authoritarian character and your mother a nice woman, patient and long-suffering. But papa said—' Here she broke off suddenly to stand and unbutton her coat and remove it. '—Papa said it was obvious Dr Bloch felt no emotional reaction, and your story of an affair was fiction.'

'Of course he would hide it!' I said.

'My father is not easily duped. But wait: without saying that *he* was the intended recipient, papa told him you'd described finding a love-letter your mother had written; and Dr Bloch chuckled and said that was impossible since your mother couldn't even write. Couldn't even sign her name! He had witnessed her Will, and one or two other documents, and she'd signed with a cross. Papa could hardly believe it, and he said he could check for himself if he cared to visit the records office in Linz. You've lied to us, Wolf, and you blackened the reputation of your own mother. How *could* you do that?'

She stopped, trembling, exhausted, drained of colour. She sat back down. I felt rage boil up in me; but also the knowledge that attack is the best means of defence. I wasn't going to let this mere girl get away with thinking she could assault me so violently, so sanctimoniously. I would *rant* back—something I know I'm good at. But I would do so as though I were performing a long speech, or singing in a Wagnerian opera; building up from an underplayed steely anger to a towering, gesticulating rage.

'How dare your father,' I began in a controlled but slightly trembling voice... 'How dare he discuss me—one of his patients—without my permission! And my poor dead mother too! Besmirching her with talk of a love-letter—no matter if *I* had done so. That was private, sacred information. No, no, please don't interrupt.' For she had started to protest. 'Dr Bloch was—is—our family doctor. He will now think badly of me, and may refuse to have anything more to do with my remaining family members in Linz. This must be a flagrant offence against medical ethics, and your father should be stricken from the list of physicians!'

I thought that was a nice touch, occurring to me quite spontaneously, and Anna looked frightened, shrinking back on her chair. I moved into, so to speak, a second theme... 'You Jews are all the same. You look after each other, because you're the Chosen People, aren't you? You pretend to assimilate, you rich ones—which is most of you—because it suits you to fill up the newspaper offices, legal offices, medical schools, and so on, thinking we won't notice, saying to us, We're not really Jews, we're good Austrians, Germans... But isn't it funny that our fat capitalists and bankers very often have Jewish names! And how many Gentile friends does your precious father have? Not many, I warrant. You create your own ghetto wall around you, then blame us for treating you as aliens! I know you don't go to synagogues, you're godless Jews, but Jewish men pray every day, "Blessed are You, O Lord, that you did not make me a Gentile." Charming!'

She opened her lips to speak but I forestalled her: '—If there's a poor farmer struggling to pay off his debts he'll be a German, and if there's a greedy swine of a collector coming round to threaten him and extort from him he'll be a fucking Jewish usurer. You grow prosperous on others' poverty. Heaven save you from ever soiling your hands! You spread disturbing, perverted ideas, whether Communist or capitalist or liberal, write filthy books, paint filthy pictures and create filthy new so-called therapies. You have to complicate everything, make everything sordid.'

Carried away by my own eloquence and passion, I stood up now and walked around between bed and piano, gesticulating. 'And your men corrupt our women. Look at that filthy engraving in your papa's waiting-room: that leering, monstrous-nosed, lubber-lipped Jew about to rape an Aryan girl. It's the Jews who seize girls and ship them off to brothels in Rio. Otto Weininger was the only decent Jew I know of, and he was so sickened by being Jewish that he shot himself—in Beethoven's house! Have you read *Sex and Character*? But how could you? Females aren't capable of abstract thought. Weininger said Jews are more effeminate than women—neurotic, weak, spineless, incapable of sports or fighting. I recall your sister laughing as she pictured your father playing tennis! They're only good for bending over ledgers short-sightedly, seeing how much money they've managed to extort since the previous day. And all the time, there are thousands more of you, streaming into Vienna— smelly, dirty, strange, inhuman with their long ragged black coats, their side-locks and sly, obsequious manner. A filthy tide. Like thousands of cockroaches. And you and your papa thought I was one of them. That's the only reason you took me home; and I was stupid enough to go along with your father when he coaxed me to say I was really Jewish; even though it meant maligning my pure, sweet, faithful mother. I wanted to please him—and then to please you too!...'

I had more to say, though I was near my zenith; but Anna had burst into tears, seized her coat and rushed from the room. Those big, desert-walking feet clattered down the stairs. I heard a bump, then silence, as though she had tripped and fallen. Just as I was wondering if I should go down and help her, I heard her descending again. I still half-wanted to go after her.

For some reason I felt tears come to my eyes. Could it be that I felt sorry for her, felt she hadn't deserved such savagery? That she was essentially a good, kind girl? Did I feel slightly ashamed? I couldn't work out how I felt.

11

I had not set eyes on her for over a week. My contact with the Freuds seemed over. I was struggling too much from my griping, growling stomach, and nightmares in which I was being choked, to worry about it much; it was all I could do to make a few sketches of the Opera house on postcards and stand out in the burning sun trying to sell them.

Then, one afternoon, a light drizzle falling from cloudy skies, I saw, not Anna, but Sophie. Clad in an elegant black coat and boots, and a grey fur hat, she was standing a few paces away from me, gazing at a poster advertising *The Merry Widow*. My heart beat rapidly: how enchanting was that pale, uptilted face, lost in reflection—*Shall I get tickets or not?* —and that graceful figure! How easy it would have been to have marched up to her, said Hello, and talked knowledgeably about the opera, which I knew well, and the artists performing it. I assumed the dull, brutish Max was due to come on another visit, and she was wondering if he would enjoy this opera. I could invite her to a nearby coffee house; I would talk eloquently, with sparkle and wit... I knew already she was charmed by me, despite my poverty. Perhaps she had been longing hopelessly for a chance to meet me again; and with this afternoon's contact life would change—her life and mine!

But I stood rooted to the spot, overcome by shyness. Just as had happened with Klara in Linz. And in a few minutes Sophie turned on her heels and walked away. Afterwards I raged at myself for cowardice. I resolved that I would create another opportunity and this time not fail.

And then, suddenly, as I stood lost in anguished thought—a miracle! I felt my arm touched, and when I came to myself, there was Sophie, gazing at me, her eyes sparkling! 'It's Wolf, isn't it?' she said.

'Yes. Hello, Fräulein Freud. How nice!'

'How are you?'

'Oh, not too bad.'

She glanced up at the poster. 'I keep changing my mind. Do you think that opera would be suitable for someone who is of a serious disposition?' She was gazing again straight into my eyes, gaily, mischievously. I was certain that she meant me, from the sparkle and mischief in those enchanting eyes.

I said, 'I am sure he would enjoy it. It's my favourite light opera, and the singers are splendid.'

'In that case,' she said, 'I've made up my mind: I shall go and buy the tickets!' With a mischievous glance at me over her shoulder she glided off, heading for the box office at the rear of the Opera.

I was aglow, certain she would return in a few minutes, eyes sparkling, hand two tickets to me and say, 'Well, would you like to escort me?' She was clearly a girl of great spirit; she might be engaged to be married, but she would not let that stand in her way if she saw a happier possibility. She, unlike Anna, would not be cowed by her father's antagonism to me.

However, she did not return, which depressed my spirits somewhat, though not entirely. It could not be easy, even for such a spirited girl as she, to cast off all convention without a qualm. She had given me a signal; it was for me, as the male, to follow it up if I wished. Yes, of course! She would fear I would see her as unfeminine and forward had she actually bought the tickets.

I took to haunting again the street where the Freuds lived: making sure there was some dark corner or alleyway I could withdraw into so that I could avoid an unwelcome encounter. Over several days and evenings I saw every member of the Freud household, including Sophie; but she was always accompanied, sometimes by her stern mother, sometimes Anna. Sometimes the mother came with another woman of about her age, or slightly less, whose face looked more animated. I assumed this was the spinster aunt whom Anna had mentioned. Dr Freud, in his lordly way, would stride out alone in the early afternoon, and return a half-hour later, having had his beard trimmed. Late in the afternoon he would emerge together with Anna; she had said this was his regular 'constitutional', walking around the Ring. And two or three times, quite late at night, he came out with a tall, heavily handsome, rather Slavic-looking lady, whom I had seen at the Donatello lecture, and who took his arm in an intimate way, all the time talking, talking, and the doctor nodding or slipping in a word, as if they were continuing a fascinating conversation.

The maid appeared often, and I had a mad idea to write a letter to Sophie and ask the maid to deliver it. It would say, 'Sophie, I know you are betrothed to another, and therefore my quest is hopeless; but I have strong feelings for you, and I believe they are returned to some extent. Please can we meet?...'

In the course of two weeks I never saw Sophie on her own, and I was about to abandon my 'hopeless quest' for good. Then fate took a hand. Anna came out walking on her own, and I thought, Better this contact than none at all. I stepped out of the shadows. 'Anna!'

Her face showed a struggle between anger and delight, disgust and relief. 'Wolf!'

'I wish to apologise profoundly. What I said to you was unforgivable, but I hope I can explain it.'

'Why are you here?'

'I've been coming here a lot, hoping to talk to you. I haven't bothered to sell a picture or even postcard since that day, and have scarcely eaten, but that doesn't matter—I needed to find you and try to put things right.'

'You have a very cruel streak.'

'I know. But this was cruelty to myself too, because I miss seeing you. I miss you.'

Her expression softened. 'I didn't tear up your picture.' A wan smile. 'I wanted to but I couldn't.'

'Can we have a coffee and talk?' I nodded towards the nearby coffee house.

'Not here, we might be seen. I'll walk ahead, and you follow at a distance.'

She found a café in a narrow, grimy lane well away from the Ringstrasse. As I sat down facing her she said, 'Since you haven't eaten you'd better have some pastries.' She signalled to the waiter. 'The marzipan and the chocolate,' she said to him, 'for my friend,' and glanced at me to confirm it.

'Thank you.' I bit into the rich marzipan, already melting on my tongue. 'This is kind of you, Anna,' I said. 'Even just to talk to me is kind.'

'Well, I missed you too. I missed you very much.' She dropped her gaze into her lap, her gloved hands fumbling together nervously. I leaned across and placed my hand over them.

She lifted her face and gazed into my eyes. 'You do have such amazing eyes! The rest of your face is quite ugly, with that squat nose—and I *hate* that moustache!'

'Ah, you can be cruel too, Anna.'

'I almost preferred your beard. Though it was rather straggly and... greasy. I remember when I touched it, to remove that bit of food. It felt... tickly. It seemed quite an intimate thing to do, to touch a strange man's beard. But your eyes... I can't decide what colour they are. Are they blue, are they green? Only my father has such amazing eyes.'

This allowed me to ask after her father, and mother, and Sophie. ('Oh, she's mooning over her precious Max. When he left last time he squeezed me rather too ardently; I don't trust him.') 'Mooning over' troubled me somewhat, but what did Anna know of her sister's real feelings? I told her I'd seen her father walking out with a tall, handsome lady. That was Lou Salomé, she said, a German-Russian aristocrat and writer. She was visiting Vienna and had become a disciple of her father. 'He's very flattered, of course, because she's beautiful and intelligent. And very bold and outspoken. Do you know what I overheard her say to papa last night? I don't know if I should repeat it, it's rather...' She became confused, stammering, blushing, lowering her gaze.

'Please tell me.'

'Well, she said, "The reception of the semen is the height of ecstasy. I want it always, constantly." Isn't that extraordinary?'

I was taken aback, and slightly repelled. A woman does not talk about such matters, even in a more delicate way. 'That sounds extremely forward,' I said.

'Oh, she wasn't flirting with my father, not at all. They were looking at a psychological paper she hopes to present, and discussing the ideas. But still, it's extraordinary, not just to say it but to feel it. She wants it all the time—constantly!' Anna shivered and her eyes sparkled. 'Would you like another cake, Wolf?'

'No. Thank you.'

'All the time! When she's eating a meal, watching a play in the theatre, lecturing!... Of course I don't know anything, and very possibly I shall never experience it. I find it faintly disgusting, actually. I certainly can't imagine papa and mama doing it. They must have had to close their eyes and grit their teeth in order to do it and create a family. I shouldn't think they've—'

'—Anna,' I interrupted, 'I'd like to talk about my offensive remarks about Jews. I don't at all—'

'—Can't we leave that till the next time we're in your room? We *are* going to meet again, aren't we?' She looked at me anxiously.

'Yes, if you'd like to.'

'Good. Because I still want to help you. And I think we were get-ting somewhere... Have I upset you? You look disturbed. Shouldn't I have mentioned sex? I know females aren't supposed to talk about it. Though papa says if a woman is inhibited from thinking about sex she won't be able to think very much at all. I only mentioned Frau Lou's extraordinary remark because—well, in this therapy it's important there should be no taboo subjects. But if it disturbs you...'

I assured her it didn't, perhaps with too much good humour; for she spread her lips into a huge smile and said, 'That's a relief! I may be only seventeen, but I have normal feelings. After all, Mary Vetsera was only seventeen, and look what she did! I've thought a lot about her, and that final night.'

We were silent for some time. I presumed both of us were think-ing of Mayerling, the hunting lodge, and all that happened there. Our spoons stirred our almost-finished coffee. When she spoke, gazing past my shoulder, she showed that her thoughts were partly in Mayerling and the past, partly in Leopoldstadt and the present: 'Poor Mary... But I'd rather her fate than my sister's. She says I'm jealous. Jealous of a man with a bald spot and the beginnings of a paunch! Far from being jealous, I am actually sorry for her. Max has almost no conversation. She is going to have to leave home, quit Vienna for dull Hamburg, where she will be bored all day, and then even more bored when he comes home, ready to be a pig at the dinner table, then puts on his slippers and drowses till bedtime. Or he'll go out again womanising.'

'Perhaps she'll come to her senses in time, and break off the engagement.'

As if she hadn't heard me she went on: 'And in five years she'll have three or four noisy infants. Her looks, such as they are, will be gone. And I'm supposed to be jealous!'

'Quite absurd.'

12

She came on an enervatingly hot afternoon and, though lightly dressed, she was panting and heavily perspiring after her walk up the stairs. I poured her some water, then made her sit still for a while to recover. Then she asked me how I was feeling, and I said, Bad, bad. The stomach, the nightmares. She said, I'm so sorry, we must get to the bottom of this hysterical illness.

Me, hysterical! But I held my tongue over that. I merely launched again into an abject apology for my insufferable outburst. 'I really don't feel at all like that about Jews, Anna. I was angry with your father, and simply spewed out the rubbish of the anti-Semitic press. I think probably the only peoples of real genius are the Jews and the Germans. The Jewish dealers have always dealt fairly with me—which I can't say about others. I've seen the culture in your homes; and you have close family lives; you go about your work peacefully, and you don't bawl and scream for your rights.'

She nodded, and rested her chin on her clasped hands in a thoughtful pose. She spoke, then, slowly and softly: 'Of course I accept your apology, Wolf; otherwise I wouldn't be here. And I have to confess your criticisms of my father were quite correct: he ought not to have discussed you with Dr Bloch behind your back. You obviously made a big impression on him, for him to do so; but it was wrong of him...' She sank her chin deeper upon her clasped hands. 'I've been thinking constantly of why you should have lied, saying you were Dr Bloch's son. Unlikely though it may seem, I've come to the conclusion that a part of you would like to be Jewish. I don't think it was a glib lie, it was a fantasy arising from an unconscious wish—a wish to be a Jew. Think about that.'

I pretended to, for a while, then replied: 'I don't think his Jewishness came into it. He was just our kindly family doctor. I contrasted his cultured voice and manner to my father's brutishness; and so—when your father started suggesting an affair between the doctor and mama, I fantasised. You're right!'

'That's very honest of you.'

'I'm always honest with you.' I could see she was struggling with the airlessness of the room, and told her I would understand if she left. No, no, she said, we were beginning to get somewhere. There were things I had brought up in my anti-Jewish... she sought the right word and I provided it: 'Rant!' and she smiled; yes, that was the word. She'd been so upset that a lot of it had passed over her head, but she recalled my mentioning Weininger...?

'Otto Weininger, yes. Shot himself in his early twenties. In Beethoven's house. Tragic.'

'I must have been only six or seven when he died, but I can dimly remember papa being very upset about his death. Why do you think he chose Beethoven's house?'

'I suppose because Beethoven is the most masculine of composers, and Weininger had this belief that Jews are feminine and weak. Which is ridiculous! Look at your father!'

'Well, papa has his tender, feminine side too. I hadn't read Weininger's book, to my shame, but naturally I've done so now. Extraordinary! The most astonishingly violent anti-Semitism, from a Jew! Jewish men are like feeble women. Something like that. How the poor man must have hated himself. Of course he was a homosexual too—did you know that?'

'No,' I said truthfully.

'I believe so. And presumably hated his homosexuality as much as his Jewishness.'

She paused, and watched me. I realised I was clasping my hands loosely over my groin—a perfectly natural thing to do—but recalling her father's insolent remark about this I moved them and folded my arms. Why was she speaking of homosexuality? Did she even know what it entailed? Not merely in the abstract way her father had dealt with it in his lecture, but the sordid physical reality? Gustl, a male, and years older than Anna, hadn't known what homosexuals did, and I'd had to tell him.

'But there's *some* truth,' she resumed, 'in what he said about Jewish men having feminine characteristics. They can be quite tender-hearted,

- 67 -

under the surface, and sensitive. They've been taught from birth to cultivate their intellect and shrink from roughness, sports, aggression of any kind. I think it can be traced back to the *shtetl* culture of the East. I remember my grandmother telling me how great a catch grandpa was, in their Galician *shtetl*: mild, short-sighted, his head always in a book, stooped, pallid! All the other girls were envious of her, Wolf! It was the women, she said, who were the tough, robust, aggressive ones. And grandma still is! I've known papa to cower before her rough tongue! It must have been hard for men, growing up in traditional Jewish homes, to adjust to life here, where steelier virtues are idealised. Don't you think?'

While musing that Jewish bankers and loan-sharks didn't strike me as particularly tender-hearted and sensitive, I said, 'I can see that.' I felt listless in the heat, and bored out of my mind. Was it a mistake, letting her back into my life? Just for the tenuous link with Sophie? But that evoked Sophie's image, and that gave me my answer: yes! However slim my chance, I had to grasp for it.

After waiting for me to say more, and shifting uncomfortably on the chair as I failed to do so, she said, 'And now, Wolf, I want to talk about that engraving, which you also mentioned in your *rant*...' Again the friendly smile. 'It's by a Swiss artist called Fuseli. I don't know much about him, but I learn that he had an influence on the Romantic movement. I've been looking at it more closely than ever before. It's disturbing—that helpless, almost-naked maiden, spread out with her arm hanging helplessly off the bed or sofa. And that leering, brutal creature perched on her.' Anna crossed her arms tightly over her bosom, as if to protect herself. She uncrossed and re-crossed her legs under her peasant-style skirt. 'The scarlet drapes in the background, and that mysterious horse's head. There's a powerful sense of evil, which you obviously felt deeply. And you saw the monster as Jewish.'

'He resembles the caricatures in the press. Which I think are shameful. Again, I was just spouting off nonsense.'

'It's called "Nightmare", Wolf—meaning that the monster is in the girl's unconscious. I had a nightmare too, the other night. I gave birth to my own dead twin sister! I woke up in a cold sweat. What I'm trying to say, very clumsily, is that we project our dark side into something external.'

'I can't imagine you have a dark side, Anna.'

'Oh, I have! And if a *part* of you believed what you screamed out about us Jews, you were angry with something in yourself.'

We were both silent for a few minutes. She was gazing into her lap. Finally she said, 'Are you angry with me again?'

'Absolutely not.'

'I'm doing this all wrong. I should have been listening to you, rather than spouting what I think… I should go. It really is too hot and stifling. But I want to invite you to something.' She blushed. 'I've been given two tickets for the Philharmonic on Friday. Knowing you love music I just wondered if you'd go with me?'

'What are they performing?'

'There's Mendelssohn. The Violin Concerto. I don't know what else.'

'I like Mendelssohn. But what would you tell your family?'

'Oh, I'd say I was going with a schoolfriend, someone they don't know: don't worry… They're good seats.'

'Well, then—yes. Thank you.'

'Wonderful!' She glowed with pleasure.

Soon after she'd left, Gustl came home. 'God,' I said, 'that girl lectured to me for an hour about the fucking Jews! And she's manoeuvred me into spending a whole evening with her!'

'You don't have to. Why do you bother?'

'It's a link with Sophie.'

'Ludicrous! She's going to be married! You don't stand a ghost of a chance. It's like Klara, you spent three or four years here in Vienna sighing for her, Adi, when she was gone, finished. You can't let go. You're a dreamer.'

'It's not hopeless. I know I'm in her thoughts. She's torn. You should have seen her delicious wink at me after the May lecture, and the seductive glance over her shoulder, outside the Opera.' Yet his words had depressed me. 'Besides,' I added, 'I'm helping this girl.'

He shrugged. 'It's your funeral.'

'Play me some *Hammerklavier.*'

He sat at the piano and crashed some chords out. I put an imaginary revolver to my temple, and mimed blowing my head off, like Weininger.

It struck me that the world is Otto Weininger at that moment. The gun is pressed against the temple.

As if by telepathy, Gustl paused in his playing to say, 'One of my professors told us today a thousand people each year kill themselves in Vienna.'

'Not enough.'

13

I had to spend an afternoon with my half-sister Geli (properly, Angelika), visiting from Linz. We had never been particularly close, and I begrudged giving up time from reading and sketching.

She said she was worried about our little sister Paula, living a miserable existence in a godforsaken village with our miserable aged aunt Johanna. Geli said she would take her herself but she was skint. Her late husband had been brutal and drunken, but at least had brought in some money occasionally. She was visiting Vienna to enquire about a debt to him that had not been paid. She'd left her little girl, also called Geli, with a kind neighbour.

Geli had been a good-looking, robust girl, and she was still, in her thirties, quite attractive, at least in body; but her face was lined and coarsened. She thought I looked starved. 'That's because I am; I'm skint too.' We were in the Prater—she wanted to be taken on the Ferris wheel, which she'd read so much about. 'I'd rather go on the wheel than have a decent meal, Adi.' 'Well, alright, if that's your choice.'

It was a cool but sunny day, invigorating. Riding at the top of the wheel, Geli clutched on to me from terror, and then as we came down we both giggled, and for a few moments we were kids again, playing in the fields. It broke the ice between us, a little.

We walked around the park, which was quite crowded for a week-day. 'Hear the Babel of different languages!' I said to her. 'Look at the outlandish, barbaric costumes! Not like the Landstrasse back home, eh?'

'No,' she said, 'but it's colourful—fun.'

'You wouldn't think so if you lived here. Riff-raff. They swarm in from their oriental shit-holes.'

Stalking near to us, an imposing, black-robed, black-bearded Orthodox priest, gigantic even without his tall black hat, tripped over his own feet. Geli giggled. And found it hard to stop. Her sense of humour has always been basic. When she had recovered she said, 'I could do with more of this, Adi. Linz is so boring. You're lucky, you moved on.'

She put her arm in mine, as she had never done before. It felt pleasing, I don't know why. We were quiet for a time then she said, 'I've got to piss, I'm desperate. Keep a look-out for people coming.' She dived behind some bushes and, before I decently moved away, I saw her hoist up her skirts and squat. 'That's the vulgar Geli I know,' I thought. A noisy hiss.

We strolled past the fortune-teller's booth. I wondered if I should tell her about her prophecy, that one of two Gelis in my life would become very important to me, but that I must be careful. I decided not to.

'Geli would love the Ferris wheel!' she exclaimed. 'When she's old enough, in a couple of years, I'll bring her. I hope she'll be alright with Helga, my neighbour. She can walk now and is into everything.'

'You're a good mother,' I said.

'I do my best. It's not easy.' Too many memories of children dying in our house, she said, not to be an anxious mother herself. But then it was easy to spoil a child. 'Your ma spoiled you rotten, she did, Adi! Always praising the Lord that He had spared you.'

I gave her directions to where the supposed debtor lived. Then, as I was impatient to get away, she became sentimental over our father, saying she still sometimes drew on his pipe to catch the tang of him. It had never been washed since the day he died. I shuddered at the thought of her sucking on it. We parted with a clumsy hug.

14

Anna and I, in two of the most expensive seats in the splendid, glittering auditorium! She was dressed-up to the nines, even to a set of pearls, and looked extremely excited. Not, I think, in anticipation of the music. I had asked her, over coffee beforehand, who had given her the concert tickets, and she had evaded the question. I felt sure she had saved up and bought them herself. Possibly even waited till after I'd said yes before buying them—trusting to luck that some would be available.

And to my enormous pleasure, the second half—the Mendelssohn being decently played in the first half—was devoted to my favourite orchestral composer, Anton Bruckner: and my especial favourite, his Seventh Symphony. It's a long symphony, and Anna yawned a few times during it; whereas my whole body and soul were absorbed in it. Tears came to my eyes in the wondrous Adagio. It moved me that a simple farm boy from my own native landscape, Upper Austria, had gone on to write such majestic music, in which one could see range on range of snow-capped mountains and lush valleys unfold.

When we emerged into the humdrum evening world of carriages for the rich, chattering nonentities who'd only attended the concert for show, and yet again the noise of some nearby street demonstration, Zionist this time, I felt even more alienated from it all. I walked in a kind of dream. Anna's voice, saying, 'That was really good', came from far away. I responded, 'It was more than really good, it was magnificent!'

'I don't want the evening to end,' she said. 'Can we go some-where?'

Rather to my surprise I found myself sitting in a crowded bar with her, drinking glasses of beer. I rarely touch alcohol—it's ruinous—and

Geli had gone from a drunk father to a drunk husband—but the German beer seemed appropriate after the Bruckner. Anna merely sipped hers, screwing up her face after each sip. But gazing, of course, into my 'amazing eyes' as I rhapsodized about Bruckner. 'He had a simple faith, Anna, and powerful feelings for his native soil. Austrian soil, but also German. There's no difference between the two. Didn't you feel that? Austrian blood, Austrian soil. German blood, German soil. He went on playing the organ in a village church year after year, with no thought of growing rich.'

'I could see you were rapt up in the music, Wolf. I liked that. You gave yourself to it completely.'

'Is there any other way?'

The growing noise of another demonstration, loud slogans I recognised as in the primitive Magyar tongue, gradually drowned out the Adagio playing in my mind. The first drummers and flag-bearers were soon passing the bar—in which most of the customers, inured to such displays, ignored the passing throng.

I burst out: 'God, I loathe this ragbag of a so-called Empire! Everyone clamouring for their so-called rights! Last week I watched some idiot from God knows where filibuster in parliament—he was into his third day—speaking in some tongue no one else understood! And then a fight broke out—right there in our precious parliament! It fills me with rage. We live in chaos. Nothing gets done.' Just then a lady of huge girth rolled her way between the tables, colliding with chairs and human backs as she went—napkins and bills fluttering down in her wake. 'Look at that enormous woman! It's disgusting! She's like the Empire, Anna! Everything wobbling! Her bosom, her stomach; I bet even her thighs hang in folds under her dress. Why can't she make an effort and lose weight? A nation has to be orderly, trim and self-disciplined, like humans.'

'She *is* quite large.'

'I've seen smaller elephants at the Circus.' She said something else but in the din from outside, as the main body of the demonstration went by, she was inaudible. When at last the unruly Magyars had passed by, I asked her to repeat what she had said. She rolled her empty beer glass around on the table. A flush rising to her cheeks she said, 'I asked you if you'd take me to see where the prostitutes are.'

'What on earth for?'

'I've never seen any. I'm just curious. I heard one of papa's colleagues say, at a lecture, three-quarters of the doctors in Vienna have their first sexual experience with a prostitute. And almost all the others have it with working-class girls—waitresses, shop-girls and so on. Perhaps papa did. I feel ignorant, Wolf. I resent being kept in cotton wool. If I'm *ever* to have a chance to make my dream come true, I have to see the lowest dregs. I don't know anyone else who could take me. Will you?'

My simple, decent sister had wanted me to take her to a park, and onto a Ferris wheel! The two contrasting requests seemed at that moment to sum up for me an entire cultural and racial schism. But I felt benevolent, after the Bruckner.

'It's not a place for women,' I said. 'Or for men either. It's why Vienna is rank with syphilis. Vienna *is* syphilis. Diseased, rotten to the core.'

But she begged, and I gave way. I led her from the glittering, electrified Ringstrasse, with its fine mansions for the rich guarded by garishly uniformed servants, into dingier, murkier, smellier side streets. Garbage and excrement everywhere. Drunks lying in the ditches. The occasional shout or scream from slum buildings, as some drunken, syphilitic man beat his wife or child. At last we reached the Spittelberggasse, passing whores in the shadows, their dead, white faces, their crimson lips. Anna seemed less affected than I—staring about her with avid curiosity. Red lamps over display windows, behind which half-dressed whores leered at us, stretching their stockings up over their thighs, seductively. I could feel, just from the sight, microbes bearing death hurtling along my bloodstream, infecting my organs, till I wanted to scream.

I walked her back to the superficially decent part of the city. She said it had been very interesting, though awful, and she was grateful. She'd never seen such places, but was glad now to have done so. Of course she knew Vienna treated the workers better than most other capital cities did: better, for example, than the London, full of fog and Fagins that she had read about in Dickens. The London, also, of Jack the Ripper. I said we had Jack the Rippers too. She kissed me on the cheek at the top of her street, and scampered off like a lively schoolgirl.

As I walked to my 'home', in an area not that much better than the Spittelberggasse, I managed to calm myself with the Bruckner Adagio, performed by a superb orchestra in my mind.

Anna did not come for our next appointment. I wondered if someone had seen us, at the opera or after, and reported her disgraceful conduct to the good doctor. Perhaps one of his younger colleagues, too poor to take a mistress yet, had been lurking in the red-lamp area! Slightly deflated and bored, I used the time to do a few charcoal sketches on cards of various Viennese landmarks, from memory. I produced six in an hour. They were, I knew, routine works, uninspired, but they might bring me in a few heller. The sightseers in Vienna would have turned aside from anything truly, exquisitely artistic. Imbeciles! I had it in me, I felt, to be... not quite a Tintoretto or Titian, but not absurdly inferior to them. But—no studio, no market, no money for paints, no great artist I could aid and learn from!

A few days later I was handed a letter by our landlady. The envelope bore a Swiss postmark. I knew no one there; wondered for a moment if some traveller to Vienna had bought a picture from me, had seen my talent and wished to support me financially. But no, to my disappointment I found, on tearing it open, it was from Anna.

'Dear Wolf,

I am sorry to have missed our appointment. You will be surprised to see that I am in a faraway place. One of my father's cousins, Eli, owns a chalet here in the alpine village of Grindelwald. He and his wife enjoy mountain-walking. They were due to go for a holiday, and mama, who has been worried about my health, insisted that I go with them. I didn't want to, but she would not back down. I would much rather have gone walking near Gastein, with papa and aunt Minna, but I presume they want their solitude, for whatever reason. There was no time to let you know. I'm so sorry.

Anyway, after a tedious train journey via Zurich and Interlaken, we are here, in a rather spartan chalet, which looks out on spectacular scenery—the Eiger mountain; the north wall of it too, which is one immense, sheer rock and ice face. No one has ever climbed it or even tried. It is unclimbable—but rather splendid to look at.

I have so far done a little walking, and helped look after their two young boys. I don't mind, I like children. But then there's Sara, a big unhappy girl of about my age. Papa thought we'd be good company for each other, but she is entirely silent and brainless.

We are to be here for three weeks. That seems an awfully long time. I miss you, I miss our talks. I hope your various ills have not been troubling you too much. I feel we were really close to a breakthrough, which makes this hiatus all the more upsetting. For me, at least.

That was such a wonderful evening! The concert—then my adventure!

Cordially yours,

Anna'

Close to a breakthrough! My God! as if this pretentious girl were a military commander!

Three days later another, thicker letter. Frau Guttman frowned suspiciously as she handed it to me. 'Who's writing you from Switzerland?'

'A rich widow, Frau Guttman, who's fallen madly in love with me.'

She prodded me in the ribs: 'Go on with you!'

I carried the letter to the nearest coffee house, which I often frequented to get warm or cool off, depending on the weather, and peruse the newspapers. I read...

'Dear Wolf,

Yesterday I had an amazing experience. The Swiss have just opened a rail tunnel which runs right up inside the Eiger, to the Jungfraujoch station. It's only been opened for a week, so I am one of the first to have this experience. We went up, up. And at the last we got out and the air was so thin I had to climb very slowly, scarcely able to breathe. Close to us, beyond the warning signs, was that sheer drop into nothingness. It made me sick even to imagine it, yet something was tugging me towards the edge. Even to jump off. Whereas normally I am terrified of heights. Have you had that strange conflict of fear and desire—for example when you have been climbing with your friend Gustl?

I imagine Prince Rudolf and Mary Vetsera must have felt something similar on that last night of their lives. The fear, the desire.

Do you mind me writing to you? It's just that I don't feel close to Eli, whom I scarcely know. He runs a business in Prague. I have even less in common with Leah, his wife. I can see it's a difficult marriage. Today at supper, he gazed over his spectacles out of the French window, at the Eiger in blackness. Was he thinking, Wouldn't it be better to be hanging in the icy blast on that vertical mountain than keep up this charade with Leah? Plump Leah, staring down, stuffed wienerschnitzel into her wide mouth, and her fleshy jowls quivered. Then there's my inner world, including my dream world. Last night I became aware of a monstrous frog, as big as a human baby, squatting on my chest. I stared in horror, unable to move any part of my body. I tried to cry out but could not.

Papa entered and stood nearby, looking down at us with a sad expression. He was sorry, he said, but at least this was *some* kind of baby. As the youngest daughter, I could not expect to marry and bear normal children; it would be my duty to stay at home and look after him and mama in their old age. I must suckle this frog and be grateful. And, indeed, it had my nose and mouth—could I not see?

Not very pleasant! But now let me tell you about a daydream I often have—a fantasy, if you like. It comes when I'm lying down, resting. There is always a great Prince, of mature age. He would never be so selfish as to take his life, as Crown Prince Rudolf did, despite his many sorrows. There is, fortunately, a young officer of the Guards who serves him with absolute fidelity and brilliance.

Thus far in my story, all is gentle and pleasant; my head on the pillow is lulled into a childlike trustfulness, almost as if a cradle song is being sung to me. But nothing is perfect. The young officer does something which bitterly offends his Prince. This is the point where I start to weave my variations. Perhaps he has stolen kisses from the Prince's beautiful daughter. Or more than kisses. The Prince is justifiably wrathful. Sometimes I can hardly breathe.

Finally, all is well. My Prince recognises the Soldier's agonised penitence, and that no one on this earth is perfect. He summons the young man to him; the Soldier kneels before him, weeping; whereupon the Prince rests his hands on his shoulders and tells him to rise; his anger has died away like a storm on a lake.

I'm tired of being a good girl, Wolf. What good has behaving nicely done me? I was not wanted in the first place: the last of six children. A moment's relapse into youthful vigour and desire. On papa's part, I assume. I am sure my mother has never felt sexual desire. I was like an afterbirth, you might say; one that came alive, inconveniently.

Well, it's late. The chalet is asleep. The Eiger is *definitely* asleep. Goodnight, Wolf. I've enjoyed talking to you: it has felt like that.

Yours affectionately,
Anna'

15

Thereafter, almost every other day, another letter arrived; and each one more crazy and shocking than the last. I read them out to Gustl, or let him read them, and he agreed she was seriously unbalanced. 'If you weren't a decent fellow,' he said, 'you could show them all to her father and demand money for handing them over.'

'But how can two sisters be so different?' I exclaimed, scrunching her latest letter in my hands and pacing up and down near Gustl at the piano. I had caught glimpses of Sophie a few times, leaving or entering her home. 'The other—well, you can just tell from looking at her sweet, unclouded face that she hasn't an impure thought in her mind. She's as pure as Swanhilde... Now let's get back to the *real* world again. 'Let's try the Wieland-Swanhilde duet in Act Two. Admittedly it's difficult imagin-ing you as my beautiful, half-divine wife, but I'll try!... Start the intro... *Diminished seventh*, you DOLT!'

Herewith a selection from Fräulein Anna...

'My dear Wolf,

This afternoon, while the others were out hiking, I lay here in my room, with the shutters closed, and went into another of my repetitive reveries. I won't bore you today with the details. Enough to say that the Prince became enraged. I felt all of his wrath within me. So great a betrayal. He says nothing for several days, nursing his hurt, brooding. Everyone can see he is out of sorts; the young officer is anxious, and begs him to say what has disturbed him.

This is the point where I become really distressed and tense myself. How can they be reconciled? The story must end nicely. That's vital.

But this time the Prince is hurt to the core of him. It's not going to be easy to forgive...

I'm sorry I can't go on. My head throbs. I will write again tomorrow.

Anna'

'My dear Wolf,

Something dreadfully embarrassing happened yesterday. I refused their pressing invitation to join them on a day's hiking around the Eiger, saying I wanted to explore around here and find somewhere to sit and read. They set off, and after a while I strolled down to the village; went into the Catholic church, where a plaster statue of their Virgin gazed down reprovingly at me, as if she were saying 'Bad Anna! Bad Jewish Anna!'

When I came back and let myself in, the chalet was of course completely silent. The maid too had gone out with them. I came upstairs to go to my room, but heard weird noises coming from the master bedroom. I was terrified we'd got a robber ransacking us. I slipped my shoes off, crept up to their door, and listened. Yes, someone was definitely in there. Very cautiously I opened the door and peered in. White wall, with a framed oil painting of the Eiger; an ornate dresser and mirror... Part of a four-poster bed next in view—and something strange, which my mind could not interpret immediately. A naked male figure, a trimly bearded head, slightly raised from the pillow... Eli—who should have been faraway!

And nestled against him, a plump female torso... his wife! I was so convinced they were off hiking somewhere that I thought for an instant I must be hallucinating. The rosy bud of one plump breast exposed above the edge of her corset. She was making strange little sounds as his body moved upon her. I mumbled, 'Oh my God, I'm so sorry!' shut the door and raced to my room, trembling and my heart beating wildly.

An hour or so later I came downstairs and found Leah in her dressing-gown, reading a novelette. I stammered again, 'I'm so sorry! I thought everyone was out, and heard noises from your bedroom. I feared some marauder.'

She reacted in a better way than I had expected—perhaps even with a shocking casualness: 'It's alright, Anna; these things can happen. As a matter of fact we changed our minds after a short while. My feet are sore, and—well, we thought this would be a rare chance to have a little time to ourselves. The boys are fine with Trudi and Sara.' Her gaze fell again on her novelette. 'This is quite good; you should read it.'

I miss you. I even miss boring Vienna.

Yours affectionately
Bad Anna!'

'My dear Wolf,

It's hard to get that flagrant image of the *coitus* out of Anna's filthy young mind! And I couple with the image (a nice verb!) the memory of Frau Lou saying to papa, 'The reception of the semen is the height of ecstasy—I want it always, constantly!'

The Prince is very angry—someone has been in his private library, disturbing his books, his papers. Even worse, has been leaving dirty hand-marks on some precious erotic pictures. The Prince is a connoisseur of art, and possesses one of the finest collections of erotic drawings and paintings in Europe.

He would happily have allowed the Soldier to look through his collection, if only he had asked permission. But to have stolen in and *pawed* the prints furtively while he was out hunting—that was unforgivable. It has to have been the Soldier who stole in; no one else possesses a key to his library. Unbelievable tension! How can this be forgiven, how can the Prince and the Soldier become reconciled after such an offence? Yet reconciliation, and a nice end, there must be…

That was the 'variation on a theme' I chose earlier this afternoon, during my siesta, after a morning playing with the boys. It took a huge amount of effort and imagination to bring about a reconciliation between the Prince and his Soldier, but there was peace at last. I had a sleep, and woke up with a real sleep-dream in my head. A fragment. Here it is… My father is dead, and I have to buy some black dress material. Filled with misery, I go to a shop called Weininger's, where I am served by an old Jew. Breasts bulge through his shirt, and he apologises, saying it's because of some illness, but he is not a woman, thank God. An Ostjew, all beard and side-locks, enters the shop, and plays a lament on a violin.

I'll admit to a little 'anti-Semitism' myself: when I see more and more Ostjews swarming into Vienna, so poor and... *primitive*, if you know what I mean, then I fear them, at the same time as I pity them. Or I fear how they may affect the political atmosphere for the rest of us. One of my few Aryan friends at school told me the Ostjews carry a peculiar smell with them always, and even their farts smell different! True or not, it makes it hard for us educated Jews.

We leave soon for Vienna, thank God. This will be my last letter to you.

Yours,
Anna'

Gustl: 'My God, Adi! How can you bear this avalanche of girlish tosh?'
'Because I'm a saint, like mama. Anyway it's over, she says.'
'I shouldn't count on it. She's bored out of her mind, and dreamy, O so dreamy, about you!'
I punched him lightly in the stomach.

'My dear Wolf,

I am shaking. It's early morning, still dark. I haven't yet got dressed. A dreadful dream.

It started normally enough. I was visiting a man I trusted and thought I knew. Some kind of teacher. Stuffy, dark room. I admired a very fine, almost transparent shawl. I asked him if I could buy it from him. He said yes, but it was very expensive, because it was made out of human skin. He was suddenly behind me and gripping me tight with both arms. I felt him rub himself against me from behind. I struggled with all my might to get free. And then I felt wetness on my dress behind.

Feel horribly oppressed by it. And there's a storm raging around that gloomy Eiger north face, and has been doing so for more than a day. Thank God this abysmal 'holiday' is drawing to an end. I'm sure they're as sick of me as I am of them. I will come to you on Monday, as before.

Yours,
Anna

ps. On a lighter note, out of sheer tedium yesterday I read Leah's novelette. It had a duel in it. I would love to participate in a duel over some woman! The thrill of… will you live? Will you die? I wonder if women have ever duelled. Do you know?'

16

I need hardly tell you that these missives went straight into the bin, once I had copied a few of them for *1912 Overture*. I had no interest in the older members of her family, and even less her tedious fantasies. Let her fantasise about Princes and Soldiers to her heart's content, but not imagine anyone else, engaged in the daily struggle to survive, wished to share them! As for the indecencies, the less said the better; she is sexually obsessed, as who can wonder with the father she has? I thank God I escaped that particular disease. I include her letters only to show how a basically decent young girl can be warped by privilege and parental influence.

During her absence, I was twice granted the longed-for vision of her (oh so much more feminine and adorable) sister, leaving the apartment building with her mother. Brief joy and enduring frustration were my only reward for cold hours in the Berggasse.

As a previous cameo suggests, I also, with Gustl's help, began my project to compose an opera, in the style of Wagner, on the subject of Wieland the Smith—an idea which had first occurred to me in Dr Freud's august consulting room. I created the libretto, in rough, and some of the music in my head; then I would sing it to Gustl and make suggestions about the orchestration. It constantly frustrated me that my own untrained piano playing was not capable of translating the glorious music into reality; and neither, in fact, was Gustl's superior, but still far from first-class, technique. And of course even had he been the world's greatest concert pianist, instead of a competent music student, he could hardly have represented the varied harmonies of strings, woodwind, brass and percussion that I could inwardly hear. But we were trying.

I had forgotten Anna was due to re-appear, *post*-Eiger, on an after-noon when Gustl was free from classes and we were engrossed in music. Upon her arrival, she was taken aback by his presence and our obvious preoccupation. I introduced them to each other, and Gustl explained that he'd had some free time, owing to a professor's absence through sickness, but would soon have to leave for another class. I asked her to take a seat and listen—that she could be our first audience! She looked tired, and was moving awkwardly. She explained that she had a painful back.

'What should we perform for her, Gustl?' I asked him.

'"Let me be free"? That's more or less finished, and it's very strong.'

'Yes, "Let me be free".' And while he searched for those sheets on the piano top, I explained the aria's background to Anna. 'He's been taken prisoner by a corrupt king, chained in a dungeon, and has to create on his anvil lots of treasures. In order to make sure he can't escape, but can still use his hands, the king has ordered that the tendons of his feet should be cut through. He's helpless. How like an artist in this corrupt society!'

I am no actor, but for me our miserably damp (autumn had set in rainily) and poky room was transformed into a hideous dark dungeon, with chains on the walls and instruments of torture. I went into a crouch, and twisted my legs, till I could almost feel the iron chains bind-ing me, and the pain of my severed tendons. Gustl started to play the introductory chords—interrupted by my shouting, 'That's an accidental, you moron!' Then I launched into 'Let me be free, let me be *free!* Let me have wings to fly away—to fly away—to *fly away*—and wreak my ven-geance…!' At the end of that aria—which should be sung by a bass, not baritone—I always felt wrung out and exhausted from the emotion of it. Anna clapped and said, 'That's very nice. You have a good singing voice, Wolf; and Gustl, you play so well!'

'Oh, not as Adi would like!' He smiled. 'He'd like the whole Vienna Philharmonic in here! But I do my best.'

'How do you put up with him shouting at you so much?'

'I'm used to it, Fräulein I've known him since we were children, and he's always shouted and cursed at me! But he's a good sort, really.'

'Yes, I know that.'

'Saved my mother from drowning. Kind to animals. Except rats. You used to love shooting rats, didn't you, Adi?'

'Let's try one more,' I said. '"O mute but glorious Folk"—think you can play that a bit better?... Anna, besides being the chained artist, Wieland is also the Folk, the people, chained by filthy capitalism.' Would I rather have Communism? she asked. 'No, filthy Communism neither. And least of all filthy Social Democracy!'

'Then what?'

'Something altogether fresh; I don't know what yet. It will come to me, if my miserable life be spared. Now listen to Wieland...'

I think we performed this aria well, and Anna clapped more enthusiastically than before. Of course I am always left totally dissatisfied and frustrated. 'I'll go to the opening night at the Vienna Opera!' Anna promised.

'Ah, what hope of that? I haven't got the contacts, the influence. And even if I did, and it were performed, it won't be as good as Wagner would have made it.'

'Oh, you undersell yourself, Adi,' Gustl said. I'm never quite sure if he is sincere or ironic. He addressed Anna: 'Don't you think he has the capacity to emulate Wagner's exalted vision?'

'Well, I'm not familiar with Wagner. I'm an ignoramus musically; but I do think he is very talented.'

'I must be off,' Gustl said; and after gathering up his coat and music case, clicked his heels and bowed to Anna. 'It's been a pleasure meeting you, Fräulein Freud.'

'Anna, please. And so nice to meet you at last.'

With a nod to me and a 'See you this evening', he left. She paid some compliments to him—he seemed nice, very modest, and so on; then, as I sat down on the bed, said, 'You received my letters?' A look which implored me to say they were wonderful, and I would treasure them. I nodded, and said, 'They were very... honest, very... frank.'

'Yes. You'd told me you wanted me to be forthcoming too, and I haven't been. It's been *me* persuading *you* to reveal more of yourself. I thought that was unfair. Of course if this were an orthodox therapy I wouldn't be revealing anything of myself, but it's not. I don't have the knowledge. So, with the benefit of distance, I thought I would write to you and show you something of bad Anna.' She smiled.

'You seemed not to enjoy your holiday.'

'Oh, it was awful! We didn't get on, I wouldn't join them in their walks. Partly because my back hurt and I was so tired. I've been tired, off and on, for months; I don't know what's the matter with me. Though I feel better today, seeing you. I missed you.'

I felt awkward; twisted my legs as though I was still Wieland.

'Well, I missed you too… How is your father? How is Sophie?'

She grimaced. 'Oh, they're both alright. Papa is getting miserable because Sophie will be leaving. He's undermining Max's character to her —half-jokingly, but he'd really love it if she broke it off. She won't; both his other daughters will have married and gone, and he'll be left with me. I'm his Cordelia.'

'I don't understand.'

She explained that Cordelia was one of three daughters of King Lear, in Shakespeare's tragedy; the only one who was loving, and faithful to her father, and sorely ill-used by him.

'Sophie isn't persuaded by your father's arguments? Against marrying this man from Hamburg?'

'No. The more he dispraises Max, the more mama praises him! She won't be sorry to have another daughter off her hands. When my oldest sister got married, mama was radiant; even at eight years old I could see that. Whereas mama was inconsolable even when my brother Martin left for university! I sometimes think, when Jewish boys reach fourteen or so, there should be a marriage ceremony with their mother and they should share the marital bed. The husband should move into the boy's room.'

She added, rather hurriedly, that of course she was joking. It was just that she couldn't imagine her parents having sex. It was unimaginable and distasteful, the very thought. 'I find it very hard, actually, to visualise *any* couple doing it.'

I said, 'But you *saw* a couple doing it! Your father's cousin and his wife.'

She flushed, and looked confused. As if she couldn't remember. Or—the thought flashed into my mind—had even made the incident up. But anyway she recovered, saying, 'Oh yes, that was *terrible*, Wolf! But I mean—I didn't actually *see* more than movement under the bedclothes. It's still mysterious to me what really happens.' She moved a hand vaguely over her lap. 'I mean, one knows all the theory, but in practice… Let's change the subject. We're talking about *me* still. You've gathered I don't have a particularly close relationship with my mother: what about yours? Papa said Dr Bloch described you as treating your mother very tenderly when she was dying. That must have been awful for you.'

I was happy to talk about it again. Happy and sad. At least, however neglectful I might have been earlier, quitting Linz for Vienna, I made up for it at the end. I spoke of how close we became then; how I didn't mind performing the most menial and intimate tasks for her; how

I'd ask every morning what food she might fancy, and went out to buy it; how I would bathe her forehead and stroke her when she was in dreadful pain; how, despite everything, I wanted to go on serving her, tending to her, even should she live for years.

Anna wept.

Up until that moment I had kept my emotions well in check; but at the sight of her tears I felt my own tears rising, first to a prickle in my throat, then behind my eyes—then I had buried my face in my hands and was sobbing my heart out.

A moment later I felt her arms surround me, and my head was being pressed to her girlish bosom. Her lips were brushing against my forehead and she was crooning words, or rather sounds, of comfort to me. I eventually got myself under control, managed to stop crying, and Anna moved swiftly back to her chair. I looked at her through blurred eyes, but also through *new* eyes. Her kindness, her compassion, had caused my grief to overflow—rather than the memory itself. 'Thank you, Anna,' I murmured; 'I'm not used to such sympathy. It touched my heart.'

She made a gesture as if brushing my thanks away. Her dark eyes, I thought, are very warm, very intelligent, very expressive; and her mouth —some would say it was rather swollen, overfull—but it was generous. I had felt those full lips brushing my forehead, sweetly. She was in a white dress, with a blue belt and blue-and-white scarf, knotted at the front. I had rarely noticed what she was wearing.

'So how have *you* been feeling, these past weeks?' she asked.

'Well, I've had a couple of blackouts, and after one of them I was blind for about fifteen minutes; and I wake Gustl up every other night with my screaming. Last night, he said, I was shouting out, "Get him off me! Get him off me!" I've no idea who *he* was. No, I've not been well. I've been depressed too. Do you know that Brueghel painting in the *Kunsthistoriches*, called "Hunters in the Snow"?' She gave an uncertain nod. 'It shows hunters and their dogs wearily dragging back through the snow to their lightless frozen village. It's so dark! Even the snow looks dark and frozen. That's how I've been.'

'I'm sorry. I've not been any help to you.'

'You have been today. I'm depressed about my future. I'm not getting anywhere, and I've no prospects.'

'Me too! We're both hunters in the snow.'

I discussed our session with Gustl that night, as we huddled under the blanket to get warm. We were sharing a box of chocolates Anna had brought back from Switzerland for me. 'She seems a nice girl,' he said; 'you shouldn't fool around with her. That coffee cream was gorgeous!'

'I'm not fooling around. I saw her as a possible way to Sophie, but that's hopeless—you were right—as hopeless as the lottery ticket I bought to get Klara. I could do worse. Her family's well off and influential.'

'But her father doesn't like you.'

'Oh, I'm sure he could get over that. A suitor, with talent, for his plain daughter. They'd probably jump at it.'

'Well... she's obviously crazy about you.'

'Yes.'

'She wants you to fuck her.' He giggled, and searched for another chocolate amid the rustling tissue paper.

'Yes. Hey, don't take that praline!'

'Up the ass.' He giggled again. 'That's what it sounded like in her dream of the old man pressed up against her back.'

I groaned and said, 'Then she can think again. Girls can be so vulgar. I had to put up with Geli pissing and shitting in front of me. If she took me out for a walk, to give mama a break, she'd find us a quiet spot in a meadow and up with her skirt and do her business—whichever it was!'

'I bet it turned you on, didn't it? Seeing her bare ass. I wouldn't have minded seeing your sister's bare ass.'

Gustl, good fellow though he is, can be very childish, as he had shown twice within moments, in relation to Anna and my sister. I turned over away from him, to try to sleep. He said, 'Don't fucking wake me up tonight with your screaming!' and I grunted sleepily.

17

Anna and I started to meet occasionally outside. Once at a free concert in the Musikverein, once to look at 'Hunters in the Snow' and other paintings in the *Kuntshistoriches*. She told her parents she was extending her cultural knowledge, in preparation for her teachers' course, due to start in the spring. She seemed to have a devil-may-care attitude to the risk of being seen by acquaintances with a young man of doubtful provenance. For my part, I would have been quite glad to have our continuing, and indeed mildly burgeoning, friendship known about. Bring it to a head. Now and then, if we were walking along a secluded street, she would slide her arm into mine—and hastily remove it if people suddenly appeared. When the moment came to separate, there would be a swift kiss on the lips, in some quiet corner. The kissing had begun, as it were, by accident, when I had planted a kiss on her full red Jewish lips to stop her from talking some psychological drivel.

On two occasions, when she was accompanying her father on his evening walk around the Ring, she spotted me ahead, trying to sell my pictures amid the usual gaggle of Ostjew pedlars. She acknowledged me with a lift of her eyebrows, simultaneously hugging her father's arm more tightly and beginning to engage him in animated conversation; diverting his attention so that they passed by without his seeing me.

Our relationship remained undefined. It was clear she was in love with me; I wasn't sure how I felt. My feelings veered wildly. I tried to sketch her, but it was not a very good likeness. The human face does not greatly appeal to me.

Like any sentimental girl, she wanted us to have coffee and pastries in the establishment where I had taken her and Sophie after the Karl May lecture: our first 'social' meeting where, according to her, we had found our views of the world were so astonishingly similar. Coffee and marzipan before us, Anna placed her elbows on the table, her gloved hands clasped beneath her chin; she leaned forward and, smiling, murmured, 'What do you remember most about that first occasion?'

'Well, there's so much,' I responded. 'I remember how intelligent and idealistic you appeared to be, for a girl still in school—much more than your sister, though she is charming.'

She pouted playfully: 'Admit it, she's far prettier than I.'

'I wouldn't say that. *Prettier* perhaps, in a doll-like way; but you have the beauty of high intelligence and character—not to mention gorgeous lips!'

'You flatter me. I know she's much more beautiful and joyous. Well, I'm afraid three or four children, and having to put up with Max playing around with tarts, will dim her sparkle. I'm not jealous of her. Papa says we are always duelling. I asked him if women had ever duelled —do you remember that in my letter?—and he said, Yes, many women have fought duels; for example, there was a French countess and a marquise in the eighteenth century who duelled over their lover, the Duc de Richelieu. Then there's you and Sophie, he said, though fortunately you have never fought to the death! He can be very amusing and droll— unfortunately you never saw that aspect of him.' She brought her hands down to touch mine on the table. 'What else do you remember?'

'I remember there was a demonstration going on. Ruthenian nationalists and Serb nationalists, I think. But when *isn't* there at least one going on? Vienna is a mad-house. All these Reds and piddling nationalists from God knows where, I'd lock them all up! And shoot the ringleaders!'

'But Wolf, you're a pacifist!'

'Pacifism is a noble ideal, Anna. And I certainly wouldn't fight for this goulash of a so-called Empire. All the same, society can't exist without discipline and order imposed from above. And that means being ruthless with the trouble-makers. I'd smash them with no hesitation.' I smashed a fist into my other palm. Her smile faded and she withdrew her hands from the table. 'I'm sorry, but you should know who I am. Sometimes violence is necessary; to smash everything and start afresh. I can be a violent person, Anna.'

'I know. I've seen it. Or at least heard it. Papa said your violence really disturbed him—especially as in so many ways he could see himself in you.'

'He can be violent too in a quiet way,' I said. 'With words.'

'Yes; if colleagues, or rather disciples, take issue with him, they must beware! His is a velvet violence, unlike yours, my dear. But then, you were taught violence by *your* father, weren't you? I remember you right here, recalling how he used to beat you when he came home drunk. And calling out the number of the blows: *Beat*—thirteen... *beat*—fourteen... *beat*—fifteen!' She indicated the blows with a slight movement of her hand in the air, rather like a conductor in a *pianissimo* passage; a faint flush in her cheeks.

'Did I tell you that then? My God, yes. I never loved him, but I respected him. He'd lifted himself up from being a village shoemaker to the rank of captain in the bureaucracy. Literally lifted himself up by his own bootstraps!' That Franz Josef handlebar moustache and pomposity. The alcoholic breath. The stinking pipe-smoke.

'Have another cake, my dear.' She signalled the waiter.

'Thank you. I have a violently sweet tooth!'

She declined another cake for herself, and while I chose one and started to nibble it appreciatively, she stirred the remains of her coffee and gazed thoughtfully into the cup. A silence; we were both busy, I munching, she stirring and thinking. At last she said, 'I'm very very lucky. I have a good home, a peaceful home. No one has ever lifted a finger against me. Far from beating me, my father still sometimes dandles me on his lap.'

It was an odd picture: the austere Dr Freud dandling Anna, seventeen and by no means a sylph. She lifted her face to look me straight in the eyes. 'And yet, there's violence in me too. I don't know why. It torments me.'

'You—violent! Never!'

'You remember I wrote you about my daydream? My fantasy of the mature, wise Prince and the loyal young officer he loves and trusts but who betrays him?'

'Yes. It's a very strange fantasy.'

'I've had it for ages. And I have it every day, unless I'm unusually busy. The exact circumstances change, but the basic story doesn't. In some way the Soldier lets the Prince down, and the Prince is distraught. They're both distraught. It *has* to end in forgiveness and harmony, or I don't find any peace. It's such a grave offence, whatever it is, there has to be punishment before forgiveness... I don't know if I should tell you.'

Dabbing crumbs from my mouth with my napkin, I urged her to continue, saying we should have no secrets from one another.

'Well, that's what I think too. Alright.' She breathed in deeply and expelled the breath with a big sigh. 'Well, often there's a sort of displacement on to a new character.' She leaned forward, and said 'Please come closer. I can't say it aloud.' There was no one else close enough to overhear normal tones, but I did as she asked, leaning forward conspiratorially.

'A new character enters the drama,' she whispers.

'A new character?' I whisper back.

'Yes. A boy. He could be one of the Prince's stable-lads, or a young relative or friend of the officer's. I usually call the officer the Soldier, actually.'

'A soldier. In the Austro-Hungarian army?'

'Oh, it doesn't matter what army! In the Prince's army, of course. Don't interrupt me, please, or I won't be able to come out with it. This boy... let's say this stable-lad... is ill-treating a tethered dog. Kicking it mercilessly. The Prince comes along at that moment. Now, the Prince loathes nothing more than cruelty to a defenceless creature...'

'Me too, I can't stand it. Sorry.'

'He sees red now, roars out a command to stop it, and the boy is terrified, turning his head and seeing the master. The Prince seizes him by the collar and drags him into a clump of trees. Tells the boy to strip naked and bend over a tree stump. He obeys, shivering. "You should feel some of the pain that poor dog felt, you wretch!" cries the Prince. Then he takes his riding-whip and lashes the boy's buttocks. I feel his searing pain too. But he deserves it. The Prince feels the pain himself, but keeps going for the sake of the boy's future life. His moral life. Again and again the whip descends. *Beat*—ten... *beat*—eleven... *beat*—twelve... Oh, there's nothing velvet about it!'

Her eyes, moist with unshed tears, are looking straight into mine. Her husky whisper continues: 'When the boy crawls away howling, the Prince feels somehow purged of his anger at the Soldier too. He will be able to talk to him quietly about it, expressing his pain at betrayal but able to say, "I forgive you, my dear friend."'

'"I forgive you, my dear friend..." Always that?'

'Yes. Or similar words. And he may put his hand on the kneeling Soldier's head. And at that point, Wolf, all my unspeakable tension clears. There's usually been a blinding headache, but now it vanishes. I feel quite blissful. My whole body is bathed in sweat. As it cools on me, so that I have to pull the blanket over me, I begin to feel shame and remorse.

'I ask myself why I can't limit myself to the nice fantasies; but it feels so much more *releasing* when I've pushed it to an extreme before the act of forgiveness comes.'

She leaned back, heaving another big sigh, and sipped the dregs of coffee in her cup. I leaned back likewise. She spoke in her normal voice: 'I think I mentioned the Virgin in the church in Grindelwald. The mother of God!' She chuckled. 'She looked down on me and definitely did not approve. She was telling me I'm an unregenerate Jewish girl... An unregenerate non-practising Jewish girl!' Her arms were trembling and she clasped her hands to still them. 'You're probably thinking the same... What are you thinking?'

'I'm not sure.' I really didn't know. 'For my money, anyone being cruel to a dog deserves a thrashing.'

Smiling faintly, she shook her head, and said I didn't understand.

'Well, then, tell me. What am I missing?'

'Do I have to spell it out?' A blush suffusing her face. 'It excites me.'

I frowned, mystified. 'But how?'

She lowered her face; then, looking up again: 'Sexually of course.'

'Sexually!'

'Yes. You know, sex—you've heard of it, haven't you?' A twisted grin on her face. 'Sometimes I... touch myself, but usually I don't even have to do that, it happens just from my thinking of the beating. It happened like that in this very place, when you described what your father did. I suddenly... was wet.'

'Wet?'

'Between my thighs. It happens to females, dear Wolf. You really are innocent. I was so afraid you or Sophie would notice what was happening, but neither of you did.'

I burst out angrily, 'My God, Anna, you *enjoyed* my memory of pain —in a disgusting way! You're... perverted.'

She winced. 'Yes. Your anger is well-deserved. Now you have to forgive me!' she cried with almost childish glee. 'Then it will be complete, I shall feel blissful. A blissful release. You understand?'

'You didn't just—?'

'All but.'

I signalled for the bill. Anna said, 'This is my treat, of course.' I said, 'In that case I forgive you!' At that, her face softened, she seemed to shudder, but pleasurably. I added, 'But I really don't understand it. I can be violent, and want to smash people, but I don't get any sexual pleasure from inflicting pain.'

'Oh, I'm not inflicting pain—the pleasure, if it can be called that, is in having it inflicted on me—deservedly.' She touched my hand. 'I could never tell anyone else that. Well, except papa.'

'You would tell him?' I said, appalled.

'I've told him. He gives me analysis, you see; I have to be completely honest. Well, except about my seeing you.' She blushed again, more deeply, like a rich sunset over the Alps.

18

The thousand-year-old Hapsburg Empire was visibly crumbling, and I rejoiced in it. Rumours of war were everywhere. The Italians hated Austria; the Serbs hated Austria, and Russia would always back the Serbs. If Kaiser Wilhelm was stupid enough to bring Germany in on the side of Austro-Hungary, then France and maybe even England would become involved. My sole reading was the two-volume *History of the Franco-German War, 1870-71*, inherited from my father. Bismarck—now there was a great leader.

It gave me a savage joy to know, or at least to hope, that the Empire would receive a blow as swift and fatal as that of the madman's knife in Geneva which struck through the equally mad Empress Elisabeth's gown and whalebone fourteen years ago. Fated, this last Hapsburg breed. I've talked to a man who had talked to a man whose cousin, a court lawyer, was actually *shown* the sacred relic of the Empress's corset, locked away in the Hofburg palace; the bloodstained hole, which is what Austria will soon be. He said her corset revealed she had an unimaginably small waist, and he'd heard the Empress had to be sewn into her riding outfit each morning. She wandered the earth on horseback. Mad, quite mad, and who could blame her, married (if only in name after the first few years) to that corpse-like Emperor? Then the grief of losing Prince Rudolf. She may have been glad to be murdered, poor lady.

The Emperor, consoled by an actress, carried on in his fixed routine. My father always praised his sense of duty, rising at 4.30 every morning for prayers, and so on. But duty to what! I have seen him occasionally on his daily procession from the Schönbrunn to the Hofburg, ramrod-straight in his carriage, surrounded by troops and horses from every corner of his ramshackle empire. He has always looked as stiff and comical as that wide white bushy moustache of his. Once, about a year ago, I thought I saw a tear drop from his sunken, time-laden eyes onto his stiff collar, but it was probably a trick of the light. I'm prepared to agree with papa that he works very hard, but in an absurd and doomed cause. Away with him and all such relics!

My worry was that Gustl would get caught up in the start of a war. He'd received his call-up for army training, so would be away for six months. I urged him to run away to Bavaria; but he's much too 'honourable'; besides, he doesn't think there'll be a war. For his last night he took me out for a meal at a decent restaurant, and we had a good man-to-man argument about the likelihood of hostilities. I told him I was going to see my gypsy prophetess again, and had promised Anna she could come too. I would write to him at his barracks, letting him know about any predictions in terms of war or peace. I drank rather more beer than I'm used to, and Gustl drank so much I knew he was secretly fearful.

Next morning we consumed the last of a parcel of buns his mother had sent him. She knew he shared these occasional home treats with me, and wished it. I was always grateful, though with a tinge of envy and thoughts of my own mother's eternal absence. Then he gathered his things together and we shook hands warmly. He said, 'We'll still finish *Wieland*, Adi—don't worry.'

'Oh, I don't care about that.' And I didn't; the mood had passed. I was preparing some pictures for a re-application to the Art Academy. Surely *this* time they would see my blazing talent.

'I expect to see you engaged to be married by the time I get back.'

'Akh, I don't know about that. Be careful.'

He picked up his battered old suitcase he'd brought from Linz, waved from the doorway, then I heard him clatter downstairs. I felt a pang, wondering if I'd ever see him again.

The sombre booth. Flickering candles. Her eyes, that looked as if they were a thousand years old, peering out at me from under her red scarf. 'Have you had your palm read by a gypsy before, young sir?'

'Yes,' I said curtly: 'by *you*, only a few months ago.'

Totally unfazed, she said in that case she would consult the crystal ball. Leaning her elbows on the small table between us, she laid her dark, wrinkled, claw-like hands on the ball, caressingly. She closed her eyes and mumbled to herself for a while. Her eyes open again, she said, 'Do you know someone called Paul? You have complete trust in him.'

I pondered for a few seconds. 'No.'

'I *think* he's called Paul. Or something like that. Or Palace... does he live in a palace? Anyway you haven't met him yet, he's in your future. I see him in a uniform, he's a soldier... with a high rank, I'd say, judging by all his medals... But I see you, and you've got an even higher rank, you're even a general perhaps, and you're furious with him, he's let you down badly.'

'This doesn't mean anything to me.'

She went on caressing the ball, lifting her face as if for inspiration. 'It will do, it will do. I think he's a Russian, or he's in Russia. You're furi-ous, you'd like to kill him, because you're very loyal and you demand loy-alty in return... I remember you now, but you're looking very different; you're not a Jew, but you'd like to be... I'm seeing your mother, she's a very nice-looking kind lady, but she's upset. She says she begs you to come and see her... Does she live a long way away?'

'A *very* long way away! She's dead. You knew that last time.'

Again, with practised skill, she evaded any admission of error: 'Dead or alive, death and life, these are just words; she wishes you to come to her.'

'Could you ask her why?'

'She says otherwise you could get into big trouble. She's crying. I can only tell you what I see in the ball. You mustn't blame me for it. She says you're really a good boy, a lovely boy she calls you, but you could be led astray.'

I gazed at the crystal ball, enigmatic under her caressing old claws, as if somehow there was my mother lost inside the ball, and wanting me to join her. The thought disturbed me, even though it was nonsensical. Now the gypsy was murmuring that she could see a crowd of people, who looked poor and tired and hungry, and they were entering some kind of shelter. 'They're being given a sliver of soap, then they're undressing, men and women and children together, and told to go into a bath-house to cleanse themselves of lice and other vermin. I don't know what this means. Something in your future. I can't see you among them, so I don't know what it's got to do with you. Does it mean anything to you?'

'Yes!' I exclaimed. 'It's the first thing you've said which makes any sense to me. A couple of years ago I was sleeping rough, then someone told me of a new shelter where I could get a bed and a bowl of soup. But when I got there, they shouted at me to strip naked and go and clean the lice off me. It was humiliating—the most humiliating experience of my life!'

Well, she said, it could be that, though she thought it was in the future. 'But it's a very strong and unpleasant memory for you so it could be that. The ball doesn't show everything.'

She asked if I had any specific questions, and I asked if there would be a war. With a grim smile she said lots of people asked her that, and the answer was yes. Lots of blood. Then I asked if I would ever marry, and she grabbed my hand and stared at my palm. Yes, she said, I would get married, but not for a long time, and also I wouldn't be married for long. And then she said my time was up, and held out her hand for payment. I told her I had a friend, a girl who was waiting outside, who also wanted to see her, and she would pay for us both. She nodded and told me to send her in.

I went out into a dazzlingly bright, piercingly cold day, a fierce wind blowing and piling up the golden-brown leaves of the Prater. The park was almost empty of people. Anna was walking up and down to keep warm. She said, 'How was it?'

'I'll tell you later. It's your turn.'

'I'm a bit scared, Wolf.'

'No need to be.'

She went in. I walked to a clump of bushes, to protect myself from the wind and the distant passers-by, unbuttoned my flies and pissed. Then I walked to a bench, where I sat and reflected on this second encounter. It had been pretty useless. I could make no sense of this 'Paul' figure, who would make me furious with his disloyalty. It scarcely needed a Romany fortune-teller to foretell 'lots of blood' in warfare. Ridiculous also to see me being promoted to a high rank—a general, no less!—even if I became a combatant. My mother... she hadn't even known she was dead, this time! Admittedly she'd sometimes warned me against 'getting into trouble'—stupid schoolboy scrapes—so that had sounded like her. But still...

She had seen, or claimed to see, that humiliating experience of being ordered to strip naked and bath, before I could be given a bowl of watery soup and a night's billet with about thirty ruffians; but that was hardly clairvoyance. It *was* odd that she'd again told me I wasn't Jewish; even though, this time, I didn't look in the least like one of those scruffy, filthy Ostjews.

In general, I thought—a waste of time. Rubbish.

Anna emerged from the booth. I got up and walked to greet her. 'How did it go?'

'I'm freezing,' she said. 'Let's find a warm café. We'll talk then.'

We walked quickly, to warm ourselves up, and found somewhere uncrowded that seemed welcoming, with a fire blazing in the hearth. I headed towards a table close to the fire, and the next moment, it seemed, I was for some reason lying down, seeing the flames flicker out of the corner of my eye, two waiters squatting over me, one of them trying to force hot coffee between my lips. I had a cushion under my head. My dazed brain then took in Anna's perfume and her soft hand stroking my cheek.

I heard vaguely, 'Drink this, comrade,' and I took in too much of the scalding coffee, and coughed. Of course I knew what had happened: it was all too familiar. I struggled to sit up. I turned to look at Anna's anxious face. 'How long was I out?'

'Just a few minutes, my dear. Are you alright?'

'Yes.'

'You can see?'

'Yes.' I stretched my hand up to a waiter. 'Help me up, please.'

He pulled me to my feet, and helped me into a chair. The two waiters, their mercy mission concluded, scampered off to see to some of the other, curiously watching, customers. Anna sat down too, and reached to clasp my hand. 'You scared me,' she said. 'Fortunately I've seen it before, and I hoped it would pass quickly, and it did.'

My head started to clear. But my voice still sounded thick and muffled to me as I said, 'It's very strange, my blackouts started just after my first visit to this shitty gypsy, and now it happened again.'

'We ought to try to find out what it was that upset you, both times.'

'Well, both times she told me I'm not a Jew. I remember the first time thinking afterwards, Well, that's a relief.' I placed a hand over hers, saying, 'No disrespect, Anna; no offence intended.'

'None taken.'

'Just because of that tale about my grandmother, in the Waldviertel, though I was pretty sure it wasn't true.'

Fresh coffee came, and the waiter said, 'You feeling alright now, comrade?'

'I'm fine. Thanks for your help.'

'No problem; have to stick together. Workers of the world unite, and all that.' He ambled away between the tables, head bobbing. Absurd tufts of hair sticking up each side a bald patch. Comrade! A fucking Red! No comrade of mine, thank you very much.

Anna poured our coffees from the pot so absent-mindedly that she spilled some. 'Do you think,' she said, 'that in a way you did wish you were a Jew? Later you made up that story to papa about your mother and—'

'I've no desire to be a fucking Jew!' I snarled—and one or two nearby, startled heads shot around in our direction. 'Sorry.'

'That's alright.'

'I've nothing against the Jews. I just don't want to be one. Now let's drop it. Tell me what she said to you.'

'She said—oh, lots of things.' She hunched over her coffee cup, clasping it between her hands. 'I have to talk to Sophie. She knew I have a sister who's going to get married and live abroad. Well, she thought it was me at first, but clearly it was Sophie. And she said she'd be happy enough but it wouldn't turn out well. She'd fall ill. Some disease. An epidemic, she said. She said, "Tell your sister to think again".'

'Really?' She nodded. 'But of course she won't take any notice. I'd pretend I'd gone to see a fortune-teller with a girlfriend, out of curiosity, but she'll just laugh at it. *I* would.'

'Still you should try.' Just for an instant, like a passing girlish fragrance, my old obsession with Sophie came into my consciousness, then vanished again. 'What else?'

'She knew I'm to become a teacher. At least, she saw me surrounded by children, but they wouldn't be my own children. She saw me living with a woman friend, sometime, but not with a man.' A slightly twisted smile. 'Because I'm mannish, I suppose; not like a girl should look.'

'That's nonsense!... I thought she was shit today. She saw me with a man too—being let down badly by a friend called Paul. I don't know any such fellow! He's a high-ranking officer, but I'm of an even higher rank! Complete nonsense!'

Her eyes brightened, and she smiled merrily. 'The Prince and the Soldier!' she exclaimed. 'Wolf, don't you see? It's my fantasy—you're going to live it out!'

'Hah! So did she say anything about us—you and me?'

'Oh yes. She said you were going to influence my life very strongly. She waved her arms around like this as she said it'—and Anna mimed an excitable conductor; 'as if implying it would be something quite dramatic.'

The tufty-haired Communist waiter suddenly planted two plates of liver dumpling in front of us.

'We didn't order this,' Anna said.

'On the house. You both look as if you can do with some hot

food—especially *him.*' He nodded down at me, winked genially, and marched off.

'You see, people *can* be kind,' she said.

'He's not paying for them. He's a Communist and knows that kindness helps to gain converts.'

Sticking a fork into a dumpling: 'You're a cynic, Wolf.'

'A realist... It's probably human liver. Some fat banker's. But it's tasty.'

19

'My dear Wolf,

I'm in bed with a feverish chill—feeling quite sorry for myself—and mama and papa have forbidden me to leave the apartment until I'm better. Which means I'm unlikely to be able to come to you on Friday. But I hope by Monday I'll be on the mend. My ex-schoolfriend Naomi is coming to see me in the morning, so I shall be able to give her this letter to post—with strict instructions, on pain of death, not to tell a soul. She is completely trustworthy. And besides, even if she were curious who I'm sending a letter to, she knows nothing about you.

Your beautiful picture is hanging in my bedroom, so one consolation is that in a way I have your presence every moment of the day and night! I'm looking at it right now. Papa and Sophie liked it, but they think it was by a stranger called A. Hitler. I thought it was best to be discreet. One day I hope I'll be able to tell them.

I suppose I caught this chill in the Prater, but if so it was worth it to have that experience. I live in a very sceptical family, and I'm not sure I believe in fortune-telling or clairvoyance, but she said many things which have made me wonder—including the name of one of my aunts, and said she is my favourite, and she is. So thank you again for making it possible. You have already given me important new experiences, including that symphony concert, and showing me what to look for in 'Hunters in the Snow' and other pictures. So I'd say *already* you've influenced my life strongly, if not dramatically.

There is something cosy about being in a warm bedroom, with a fire burning, and even though you're coughing and sneezing, as I am, you know what it is and it will go; whereas for so much of this year I've just

felt vaguely unwell and 'down' in spirits and not known what it is. I
know that you have felt a lot worse, poor man, and yet you don't com-
plain. And those horrid blackouts, they worry me.

But I think I *may* have hit on the answer—or one of the answers—
to why these are happening! It's not yet completely clear in my mind, so
I'll keep it till we meet. I'll just say that you were relieved, twice, to hear
the gypsy say you're not Jewish—but then each time you suffered an hysterical attack. Fortunately this last time a mild one.

Mama has just brought me some chicken soup, and I had to hide
this letter under the bedclothes. I'm not sure I have the appetite for it,
but I must try, to feel stronger. I shall see you on Monday, my dear, all
being well.

> Yours affectionately,
> Anna'

The letter irritated me, with its coy holding-back of some kind of
'revelation' about me. I also reflected that she was being fussed over by
her mother and a maid, so that she could luxuriate in a brief and not too
severe sickness. No such luck if *I* got sick. I could have wolfed down
that chicken soup! My mouth had flooded at the mention. The bourgeoisie have it coming to them! One day, one day…

That thought occurs to me most strongly when I am trying to sell
my work during the late morning's Corso. I come early to get a decent
position, somewhere between the Opera and the end of Akademi-
estrasse: that area of soft luxury in the form of café terraces, the most
prestigious shops and the opulent Hotel Bristol. Along the whole length
of it, up and down, the rich of Vienna slowly stroll, parade, show themselves off to the opposite sex. Or no doubt sometimes to the same sex.
Everyone seems to know everyone else: and why shouldn't they, as they
know themselves to be the only persons of consequence in Vienna.

I sometimes wonder if everyone knows everyone else in the Bib-
lical sense of knowing; for never has there been such a heady atmosphere
of flirtation and seduction; of male eyebrows lifted aside at some beauty,
her breasts pouting and, in warmer weather, exposed almost to the
nipples. And the beauty responds to the eyebrow lift with a light smile or
a flutter of her fan. Then there are heel-clicks and the kissing of soft
white hands, the exchange of whispered words and greeting cards. I
once observed an assignation made right in front of me. Probably thinking I was a new arrival from Galicia or Russia, knowing only Yiddish,

they spoke clearly—and insultingly—in German. The white-uniformed officer had picked up one of my watercolours and was showing it to a silk-gowned, opulently-bosomed Frau. I heard him say, 'Would you give me your opinion of this, Frau Kollmann? You know more about art than I do.'

'The technique is rather primitive. One prefers a little more... finesse...' She fluttering her eyes at him... 'Whatever the art that is being practised.'

'I entirely agree. Finesse is essential, for me too. One finds it so rarely.'

Much more of the same. Then whispers; and before they parted he had flung the picture back at me.

Yes, my blood boils during the Corso.

Monday came, and with it Anna. She looked sickly, her hands when they gripped mine clammy, and a feverish glow in her cheeks. She admitted her mother hadn't wanted her to leave the house but she had insisted. She was shivering and coughing, and kept her warm coat on. Still gripping my hands she pulled me to sit on the bed beside her, gazing all the while into my eyes.

'Listen to me very carefully, dear Wolf,' she began. 'You may think what I am going to say is nonsense, the ravings of a naïve girl too much under the influence of her father. But this is what came to me when I was lying in bed sick... You are a very tender, loving man, Wolf. You showed that in your care for your dying mother, dealing tenderly with her most intimate needs—the kind of caring more common in a daughter than a son. And you spoke so lyrically and affectionately of your night with Gustl, in a mountain hut during a thunderstorm: how you warmed each other with your own bodies. You must be missing him.' She glanced towards the piano, almost as if she saw his wraith sitting there.

'Yes, of course. Where is this leading to, Anna?'

She pressed her finger to my lips. 'Wait! You idealise women, I believe. Your mother, and that girl in Linz. And you were so upset by that engraving in papa's waiting room—Fuseli's "Nightmare". It was as if you identified with the pure-looking girl lying under the leering monster. You even imagined you were Mary Vetsera, being borne along by papa and me, just as her corpse was by her uncles. And recently you dreamed you were in her coffin.'

She had a bad coughing fit, and I told her she would soon be in her own coffin if she did not take more care of herself. I made her lie down on my bed while I sat beside her, holding her hand. Her coughing over, she continued:

'My dream of Otto Weininger with female breasts should have given me a clue.'

'A clue to what?'

'You remember he spoke of Jewish men being more like women. Soft, sentimental, emotional.'

'So?'

She was silent for a while, licking her lips as though unsure how she was going to express her thoughts.

'Out with it!'

'Alright. This is difficult. Please don't take it the wrong way... You said that Jewish men pray every day "Blessed are you, O Lord, that you did not make me a Gentile." During your rant that awful day. But they don't, Wolf; they pray "Blessed are you that you did not make me a woman." Papa always says to look out for mistakes, as they can be revealing.'

I let go of her hand, to wipe the clamminess off onto my trousers. She clutched my hand again and rubbed it in her palm, tenderly, as if to soften a coming blow. She continued: 'You were confusing race and gender. And also reversing it. Since Jew equates with female and Gentile male, your mistake expressed your own unconscious wish, your inner-most self: Blessed are you, O Lord, that you did not make me a *man!* Do you see?'

'I see that you are feverish, Anna.' I wiped her forehead with my grubby handkerchief.

'When the gypsy told you you were not a Jew, you interpreted that as not a woman—which of course was a relief, on the conscious level.' She now joined her free hand to the one rubbing mine, in an excess of tenderness. 'But at the unconscious level you were upset, as you want to be more like a woman—more tender and loving—hence your subsequent hysterical attacks.' She had a triumphant glitter in her eyes as she added: 'And by the way, your choosing Wolf as your fictional name shows how strongly you fight against your true self!'

I still admire the way I kept my temper in the face of such insult-ing gibberish. I said, 'Are you trying to tell me I wish I were a woman?'

'I think so, dear Wolf. Or at least more womanly. After all, why should you prefer to be one of those aggressive, ramrod-straight Guards-men, or members of fencing clubs, without an ounce of softer feelings in them? We are all a mixture of both sexes.'

'I can assure you that I am not.'

'Well, I'm just a stupid girl. Who, if I'm honest, would prefer to have been born a male.' She gave a weak, wry smile. She pulled herself up on the bed, now sitting beside me again. 'But—well, there is another indication of ambivalence in you, my dear. Sometimes when we are talking your hands go to your lap, as if you wished... wished you were made differently there. And... well, you have quite girlishly narrow shoulders and quite broad, almost childbearing, hips. You fight against your repressed desire by being aggressive, but—'

I could restrain myself no longer. I slapped her face, hard. She burst into tears, got up, holding her hand to her cheek, and hurried towards the door. I jumped up and seized her by the arm. 'Anna,' I said, 'I apologise for striking you. One should never strike a female. But really, that was the most appalling nonsense. And deeply offensive. I will get over it. But we should not meet for a couple of weeks. Give me some time to cool down. Besides, you need to stay indoors and get yourself really well. I ascribe a lot of that nonsense to fever. Now go. Come back two weeks from today.'

'Yes, alright. I'm sorry.'

I kissed her watery cheek, then with a hangdog look, her face lowered, she left. A moment later she came back. 'I'm afraid I need the toilet,' she said; 'can I use the one down the corridor?'

'I wouldn't if I were you; there's a rat in the water closet.'

She shuddered. 'It's fairly desperate.'

'Go in the alley. It's dark, you shouldn't be seen.'

When she had gone, I chuckled grimly, imagining the genteel Fräulein Freud hoisting her skirts, squatting, and pissing—or even more —oh my God!—in the dark, smelly, rat-ridden alley. After that I seethed for a few minutes over what she had said to me. Then I chuckled again, more jovially, from realising the utter, crazy absurdity of her so-called theory. It was because she was sick, and craved desperately to show her father she was capable of intelligent, masculine thought. I wished Gustl were present, so I could tell him. I saw him chuckle on the piano stool, then laugh so hysterically that he fell off it backward. He couldn't stop laughing, while I added further details, until he cried, 'Please, Adi, no more, I've got a pain in my stomach, I can't take it!'

20

I was in dire straits. One day an old Jew looked at a watercolour I had done of the Schönnbrunn Palace and said, 'Not bad. Not bad at all, young man.' Tipping his spectacles down and looking me over with his twinkling eyes he added, 'I think I can take this.' I felt the picture was not much good, and I suspected he only took it out of pity for my gaunt appearance. I stammered my thanks. Yet there was humiliation even in a stroke of good fortune. I loathed waiting in hope while someone with power and riches weighed up a work of mine. In some ways I preferred a curt, swift dismissal—'Sorry'—to a sale I suspected was achieved partly from the purchaser's kindliness, for which I had to be humiliatingly grateful.

The money was swallowed up immediately in the month's rent. I had to pay Gustl's share now too. I knew he would pay up when he returned, but that was several months away. The old skinflint of a landlady wouldn't give me a reduction. Another lottery ticket came and went the same way as the one in Linz. An expected sum of money from my father's estate failed to arrive. I was forced to take work as a porter at the railway station, humping rich people's trunks and suitcases, I was too tired and hungry to bother with my appearance, and I felt myself slipping back into the Ostjew.

I decided to go and visit my aunt Johanna, my mother's sister, who lived with my young, rather stupid sister Paula about thirty kilometres north of Vienna. I would plead for money—of which I knew she had plenty. Mama would want her to help me. I got there by a mixture of train, a lift on an ox-cart, and walking.

A mean hovel in a mean village, under black, threatening cloud.

On the road no people, only mangy dogs, cats and chicken. I lifted the latch and entered, calling, 'Hello, aunt, it's me! Adi!' I reeled back, at the overwhelming smell of urine.

'Oh, it's you! Why have you come? You want money, I suppose; that's the only reason you would visit your poor old aunt... You look dreadful, all that hair... And that filthy coat—it looks like what the dirty Jews wear—what do they call it? A kaffir, or something.'

'It's an old frock-coat someone gave me. Beggars can't be choosers. I can't afford to keep myself well-dressed and well-groomed, aunt.' I shouted it, because she was very deaf, although she always refused to acknowledge it.

'Huh, you're just too lazy. I daresay you spend most of the day in bed, like you used to. Drove her to an early grave.'

I could see nothing of my mother in her. A humped back, a big wart on her chin, bristles on her upper lip. Ugliness, and all around her, squalor.

'I came to see you, auntie,' I bellowed; 'you and the kid.'

'Paula? Oh, you won't see her. She's out skivvying.'

'You've put her out to work?'

'You're out of work?'

I shouted louder. 'No, Paula. You've made her go out to work?'

'Well, I can't keep her. I've no money. Your father should have provided for her. He spent it all on fancy women, he did. Your poor mother should never have married him. All the wives he'd had...' And so on. Interrupted by agonisingly slow movements as, gripping hold of two sticks, she pulled herself upright to totter, with the same provoking slowness, to the door, to lock it. 'Those gypsy thieves, you can't be too careful.' Followed by the same agonisingly slow return journey, and lowering into her chair. Then: 'So what are you doing with yourself?'

'Trying to earn a living by selling my pictures. And doing odd jobs for people. But I was hoping that—'

'—You're just a layabout, you are! Your poor mother would turn in her grave, seeing you like this. It's because you lazed away your time at school.'

I looked around me desperately. I knew there was money, stuffed in jars all around the house. A morbid picture of Christ with his heart torn open gazed down at me. What work had he done, I thought: you never read of him planing wood for his father. 'I haven't been well,' I said. 'Very bad stomach trouble. I'm afraid I may have a cancer. If you could only—'

'You're afraid you'll die, just like your mother! Because you're frightened you'll go to hell. For all your sins.'

'What sins?'

'Well, for one thing, letting your mother be treated by that doctor. He killed her, he did.'

'He didn't kill her, auntie. He tried his best.'

'Look at you—no flesh on your bones. Well, I've got nothing to feed you with. You should be bringing me money, to help with your sister. That's what your poor mother would have wished...'

After that she seemed to mellow slightly, and asked me to bring some milk from the pantry. As we drank it I shouted, 'You remember my friend Gustl?' She nodded, and I tried to have a normal conversation, telling her we had been sharing a room, he was doing well with his musical studies, I had accompanied him to some grand houses, meeting some influential people and so on. Only I was held back by my shabby clothes. I needed at least another coat, shirt and shoes. She went on nodding, in between lowering her moustached and trembling mouth to suck in the milk. Then she said, 'Do you ever hear from that pal of yours—Gustl, I think his name was?'

I was sure she'd heard me, and was being deliberately provoking. I just replied, 'Sometimes.' She seemed to hear that perfectly well, as she said, 'He should have stuck with upholstery, he'll never make a musician. No ear for it. You've got a very bad cold, your voice is hoarse.'

'It wasn't, till I started shouting at you, you old witch,' I said quietly.

'Perhaps he didn't kill her. Bloch. The quack Jewish doctor. He and your mother were very... thick.'

'What do you mean?' I shouted.

'Close. I'm saying nothing.'

'Tell me!'

'I've had my thoughts. You look very Jewish.'

I began screaming at her but she had begun to snore, lying back in her chair, her head back further still, her mouth wide open and toothless.

I had just read—or rather skimmed: an intelligent man doesn't need to read more than a few hundred words of a book to take in its gist —a Russian novel called *Crime and Punishment*. It's a story in which a young, talented but penniless student murders a useless old woman for her money. Seething, I thought of doing the same. It would be so easy. No one had seen me come. Just some thieving gypsy had clobbered her... It had begun pelting with rain outside, so no one would be out

- 109 -

when I made my departure, with whatever loot I could find. One blow with the poker and it would be done. My sister Paula could take over the house. I picked up the poker.

But in the end I couldn't do it. I have a moral sense. That student was a Slav, not a German or German-Austrian. I scribbled a short note for Paula—but then, as I was about to leave, the door was burst open and a drowned rat appeared, in the shape of Paula herself. She stared at me as though I were an apparition, then, with a broad smile, cried, 'Adi!' and rushed into my arms, wet to the skin as she was. 'Paula!' I greeted her; and almost in spite of myself I was pleased. This was real family at last.

I held her at arms' length, partly to be rid of the wetness and partly to look at her again. We hadn't met since mama's death, five years ago. She was now a young woman with breasts. Except her figure was like a sack of potatoes, and her face puddingy, though still wreathed in a joyous smile. She was not much younger than Anna—but oh, the difference in poise, intelligence, confidence! Solely through education and culture. I regretted referring to her as stupid. Rather, she was a good-natured girl who had needed a hand up—which she had not been given. I felt touched by her joy.

'Go upstairs and get those wet clothes off!' I ordered, and obediently she did as she had been told. Aunt Johanna slept and snored on regardless. The trump of doom wouldn't have awakened her.

When Paula came down, wearing a flannelette nightdress, we talked. She was milking, scrubbing and washing for a farmer about a kilometre away. Then she would come home to our aunt and have to make her supper and clean up. She was unhappy and often cried herself to sleep. 'Can't you have me with you, Adi?'

'I'm in one tiny, stinking room, Paula, and I can't even feed myself. I gave over to you my half of father's pension.'

'But it's tiny, and she takes it.' She nodded scornfully towards her snoring aunt.

'I wish I could help. One day. Any boyfriends who might take you away from here?'

'Don't get the chance. You? Any girlfriends?'

'Well, there's one girl, but she's Jewish.'

'Well, so what? We're Jewish. Part. Quarter.'

'What do you mean?'

'Mama told me. Father told she. That's why they never said nothing against the Jews.'

'Shit.'

And then we talked about the early days, when we would play cowboys and indians and she said I was always the Big Chief.

We had just one dissonant moment, when she said she was so unhappy she might as well move to Vienna and work on the streets. I soon disabused her of that idea, but promised to show her decent Vienna some days soon. As I left her, with a hug and kiss, she said sadly, 'We wasn't much of a family, was we, Adi?'

'Well, dear, what *is* a family?'

I reflected, as I began to trudge back towards the city, that Paula's life, though painful, was real, as mine was—unlike Anna's absorption in fantasy and herself.

Speaking of *Crime and Punishment*, it irked me that I could not sell it, on account of its dedication on the fly-leaf—which was the main reason it was of some value! The book was rather handsome, bound in leather, a German translation of the original. It had come into my possession in the following way. As I have previously mentioned, sometimes Gustl, as a member of a good student quartet, was invited to wealthy houses where a *soirée* was to take place; he was sometimes allowed to bring a friend, and one such occasion had occurred a week or so before his departure. The house belonged to a rich Jewish banker. I have to admit it was a splendid, glittering evening, with lavish food and drink and much cultured conversation. For Gustl and me the greatest pleasure was to be allowed to roam at will in the host's magnificent library. Only the busts of Beethoven and Goethe looked down at us as we examined, goggle-eyed, the complete scores of the operas of Wagner, Gluck, Verdi and Mozart.

On our way home I had shown Gustl the book which I had appropriated. He was incensed at my having purloined the book from a host and hostess who had been immensely hospitable and tolerant of our shabby attire; but as I said to him, 'They will never miss it. It was just one of thousands. They have so much and I have nothing.'

We had found that the novel was inscribed, with words expressing affection, to the lady of the house from Natalia Stolypina—no less than the widow of the recently assassinated Russian prime minister. That made it quite valuable, we believed, but also, alas, impossible to sell.

Following my miserable failure with aunt Johanna, I went back to my infinitely tedious and physically demanding work as a station porter. It was hard to drag myself out of bed long before dawn morning after morning. And for what? Mere animal existence!

On a wet, chilly afternoon I was on a platform as the train from Munich drew in. The doors of first-class opened, close to where I was, and some grandees climbed out. Among them, from one of the compartments, came a party of three expensively-overcoated greybeards and a handsome, heavy-bosomed, middle-aged lady in a fur coat and hat— Frau Lou. She signalled for a porter, and three or four of us started forward. Then I saw, at her side, the unmistakably grand, though short, figure of Dr Freud. I saw him stare at me—pause in mid-step—and suddenly stagger, before crumpling to the floor. Great exclamations! His companions crowding around him, the men kneeling, the handsome lady crouching (all but toppling over from the weight of her bosom), trying to assist him up, while other people came running. I froze to the spot too; then went to help another passenger struggling with a heavy suitcase.

As I walked with him I glanced over my shoulder and saw Dr Freud getting to his feet and being wiped down and fussed over by his anxious entourage. By the time I returned to the platform they had all vanished and good order had been restored.

I felt certain he had recognised me; and for some reason this had caused him to faint. How absurd, I thought, that I could ever have imagined marrying into that family! I don't know how Jews organise their weddings; but if he led one of his daughters up the aisle, the idiot might fall in a faint on reaching the nervous bridegroom! A very poor start for us that would be.

21

A rather more agreeable contact with the Freuds was a missive from Anna containing a note from her together with a dress circle ticket for Wagner's *Tristan* at the Opera. Her note read:

'Dear Wolf, I hope this will express in a form you will like my profound regret for having upset you with my ridiculous, fever-fed notions. I had some birthday money, and as I am confined to the house with a wretched influenza, I could think of no better way to spend it, and asked a friend to buy the ticket.

I hope you enjoy the performance and that it will make you think more favourably of

Your sincere friend
Anna'

I duly went to the opera, a scruffy, unshaven, scarecrow figure among the plump, dapper, rosy-cheeked layabouts pretending to like five hours of opera. The music was a joy, as ever, and the great *Liebestod* swept me away, if only for a short while, into supernal realms.

I walked out to the garish meaninglessness of the Ringstrasse's streetlamps, the roar of its traffic and the row of motor cars and carriages, with liveried coachmen, ready to take the master and mistress back to their sumptuous town house. And then perhaps the master to his kept courtesan. I stood still for a few moments, dazed, blinded—but only metaphorically. Past me streamed my fellow 'opera lovers', in couples and small groups, chattering, gabbling, laughing; the Christians among them, for the most part, feeling they had saved themselves five thousand years in *post mortem* Purgatory by enduring these five hours of earthly purgatory; the Jews, for the most part, gratified that they had assimilated so much into Germanic culture that they could endure such a torture and even perhaps enjoy the odd tune.

I felt, standing there as if petrified, indescribably lonely and alone. I missed Gustl; I would even have welcomed the presence of Anna. But I had no one. No one to love and be loved by. No *Liebestod* for me.

Then I heard a voice, to my left, say, 'Herr Stiedler?'

I turned my face, astonished. I saw a tall, lean man in a dark cloak and top hat, smiling at me. 'It is Herr Stiedler, isn't it? A friend of the musician Kubelik? We met at the Ecksteins's *soirée* and had—at least from my point of view—a very interesting conversation. Oscar Grün— do you recall me?'

'Ah, yes, of course!' I offered my hand and he shook it warmly. He had been sitting opposite us at the lavish supper which had separated, for more than an hour, the student quartet's Schubert from its Mozart. A journalist—a print-Jew—and for one of the most liberal newspapers; but, in spite of myself, I had been impressed by his natural, unsnobbish way of conversing with us, as equals. A middle-aged man of wide culture. I was truly pleased to meet him again, although aware I looked very much less 'savoury' than on that evening, when Gustl had insisted I spruce myself up as best I could.

'Wasn't it inspiring?' he said, nodding back inside.

'Yes. Wonderful!'

'Look, I'm on my own, as you appear to be. I'm too excited to go home to a lonely bed, without having the chance to talk over that production with a fellow Wagner-lover. Would you do me the honour of joining me for a coffee and dessert? I know a quiet coffee house near here.'

I said yes, I would like that very much. Herr Grün said Good! touching my arm; and that he would tell his coachman to wait here. He strode off and I saw him do just that. Returning, he guided me, with a light touch on my elbow, in the direction he wished us to take. It was a bitterly cold October night, the icy wind was piercing through my thin frock-coat. It was such a pleasure to be seated, very soon, in an alcove of a warm, bustling coffee house. He doffed his purple cloak to hand to a waiter, and under it he was wearing a suit all in gold and white. Silk, I assumed. I said I would keep my coat on for a while; I was still shivering.

I could see, and also remember, his face clearly now. It was fine, like the face of a Christ by El Greco, and also somewhat harrowed-looking; but what was most striking were his friendly smile and twinkling blue eyes. We launched straight away into a discussion of the production and performers: the wonderful Tristan, the slightly too weak Isolde. I said nothing could equal the production by Gustav Mahler, in my first year in Vienna. He winced, and said he had been abroad on an assignment that year, so unfortunately had missed it. I said, 'You look as if you have been abroad recently, and in a hot country: you're very suntanned.'

'Yes.' He looked down rather mournfully at the table, at his glass of schnapps. (I had declined.)

'You look as if it was not a happy trip, Oscar,' I said.

His gaze lifted to meet mine. 'It wasn't, Wolf. I was visiting German South-West Africa. I heard the most terrible story from some of the more sensitive settlers. I don't think it's a story I can tell to my readers. My editor wouldn't allow it. Too... disturbing in terms of international relations.'

'Can you tell me?'

He sighed. 'It must go no further. The Germans butchered almost the whole of the native tribe, men, women and children, driving them into the desert and not allowing them back; and poisoning their wells.'

'That is... draconian,' I said.

'It's an atrocity. Of course as a foreign correspondent I witness or hear of many horrific crimes; but none as bad as this. I don't know what to do with my knowledge.'

Such was his obvious depth of feeling on this issue that I held back from saying what was in my mind: such as, that these were an inferior race; that the law of life is survival of the fittest. In any case he now proceeded to describe to me in such great detail what had happened to the native tribe that I could not prevent a wave of pity running through me. He took me aback, at the end of his impassioned address, by saying, 'What do *you* think?'

'It's so difficult. Germany needs colonies, if it is ever to catch up with England and France... But of course that doesn't justify... I really don't know... Let's suppose... let's suppose Herzl's dream comes true, by miracle, and you Jews one day have your chance of a return. Next year in Jerusalem! But there are too many Arabs in the way. What would you do?'

His eyes flashed. 'I would hope we would not force them out into the desert or poison their wells! Jews could never gain land by terror and slaughter. If we did, we would truly be cursed forever, for we are the righteous people—that's our only strength. Anyway, it will never happen. We are Germans, or Austrians.'

He was not a great admirer of Herzl, he added. Had I read his novel *The Old New Land*? Well, no, I had thought it more important to read Homer's *Odyssey* and Dickens' *Pickwick Papers*—though of course I did not say that. Often, he went on, an author reveals more of himself in fiction than in a factual work; and in his novel Herzl had described the present inhabitants of Palestine as being despicably rural and backwards. 'He called them dumb beasts, Wolf!' His face seemed to darken and grow mottled. 'Dumb beasts! That means you can treat them like cattle —as the Germans have treated the African natives! You can eject them or kill them and just move in. God in heaven, no! no! no!'

I was startled by his passion. He had to stir his coffee many times while he calmed a little. Then he continued, 'Oh, I'm sure our financiers could buy off the Ottomans: they're on their last legs. But what then, my friend? I am weary of seeing humanity divided into worthy people and dumb beasts. I can't stand it. We're all human, we all have souls.'

'I understand,' I said, though really I didn't, I thought his concept deranged—Aryans and Hottentots, no difference!

'I know you do, I felt that when we first met.' There was a gloomy silence on his part; a waiter came up and asked would we like anything else, and he waved him away. I felt that he might have asked *me*. But instead, when the waiter had gone, he said, 'Let's lighten the mood. None of that is going to happen, thank God. Why not come home with me for a private supper? You look terribly thin. I live alone. You could stay the night, stay many nights. I find you very congenial, Wolf.'

I was startled yet again, but this time it gave me a queasy feeling. Didn't know how to react. But when he stretched a hand across the table to touch mine, and then squeezed it, I leapt to my feet, stammering, 'Thank you but no', and rushed out of the coffee house.

Depression laid its heavy cloak on me again as I trudged back to my lodgings. This whore Vienna, this den of corruption.

Moreover he had squeezed my hand. Who could tell where his hand had been, who or what it had lately touched? In Africa, or here among his sordid clique of perverts. I washed my hands for a full hour, and still didn't feel clean.

Despair, despair. Mama, mama, where are you?

22

One morning at the station I was humping a heavy suitcase alongside a portly, spectacled man in his thirties when I saw Sophie ahead of us, smiling a welcome. My heart skipped a beat. Though well covered up to protect from the cold, she looked as beautiful as ever. She and the portly man surged together, hugged and kissed. While a coachman took over the suitcase the portly arrival pressed a coin into my hand but with eyes only for her. I was a non-person to him, a Hottentot, as indeed I was to all travellers. Sophie's gaze flitted over me, without recognition. And then they were gone, chatting gaily.

Following that second Freudian encounter I had had enough of portering. I did not so much lose the job as throw it away—hanging back, acting surly. I returned to trying to sell my pictures on the Ringstrasse. Better to eat only every other day than continue the constant humiliation.

Shortly after, I came back to my lodgings in the late, dark afternoon, lugging my bag of unsold pictures and postcards, and as I wearily trudged up the stairs I smelt kerosene. I wondered if, for whatever reason, Gustl was back from the army, and my steps quickened. But when I opened my door and entered, I saw it was Anna. She was lying on the bed, still in her overcoat. I had quite forgotten this was the Monday when I'd told her she might resume her visits. 'Oh, hello!' I said curtly.

She sat up on the bed, and said in a frightened voice, 'Hello, Wolf. I let myself in.'

'I can see that.' I could also see, even in the faint glow of the kerosene lamp, that she looked gaunt. Her eyes seemed larger than before

—the eyes of a starved rat. She was clutching her overcoat around her. I said, more gently, 'You'd better make yourself at home then, take your coat off.'

'No, I'm alright.' But the look of fear in her eyes made me suspicious. 'Are you hiding something under it?' I said.

She opened her coat, to reveal a large black notebook. My journal! My struggle! 'Don't be angry,' she said quickly; 'I was curious. I haven't read more than a few pages.'

'How dare you! How *dare* you!' I grabbed the precious book from her. 'Have you not the least sense of what is private?'

'I read very little. I would have stopped. Only I saw it was about us. I'm really sorry I wasn't Sophie when I came to you at the hostel. But of course I understand; she's beautiful and I'm plain.'

I thought quickly. 'I'm writing a novel, Anna, not a diary. Of course one uses events in one's life, but also you have to fictionalise. That was a piece of fiction. Later, when I prepare it for publication—in a few years' time—if I am spared—I shall call you, I don't know, Brunhilde Gugenheim, perhaps. And it may be an entirely different city, and your family in banking. Or dentistry. Yes, I could black out, smash my teeth in the fall, and your father could fix me up with dentures!' I managed to grin and scowl at the same time. 'But just for now, I can only see you as Anna. My dear, familiar Anna. If I called you Brunhilde it would be distracting to me in the process of creation. Do you understand?'

She pondered; then smiled. 'Yes.'

'Good! But you are avoiding the issue. What you have done, reading my work without permission, was disgusting, truly disgusting!'

'I know. I do disgusting things. Do you want to beat me?'

'No, I *don't* want to beat you!' I shouted. 'I don't want to *touch* you!' I stormed around the room, telling her just what I thought of her. She started to rock to and fro, gabbling something to herself. When I stopped shouting to find out what she was gabbling, I heard, 'A child is being beaten. A child is being beaten…' over and over.

'What on earth do you mean?' I snapped. 'No child is being beaten.'

'I am. Inside. For my sins.' A weird echo of what my evil old aunt had said, not long ago: 'You're afraid you'll go to hell, because of all your sins.'

'Well, you're certainly a liar! I don't for one moment think you saw your brother and sister-in-law making love, did you?'

'I'm not sure. I *think* so.' Said with the sly, naughty smile of a five-year-old girl. Females have a very dubious relationship with the truth. She went on: 'He might have been sleeping with a local girl; I didn't see her face, not clearly. With his wife's knowledge. She may no longer want sex. Couples come to all sorts of strange arrangements sometimes. She might have preferred reading a cheap romance, while her husband had his fun upstairs.'

'That's rubbish!'

She shrugged. 'Perhaps. Or it could have been Sara, his daughter. He's forced himself on her; that's why she looked so unhappy.'

'That's even more disgusting.'

'I'm sorry. Bad Anna.'

'Stop that rocking to and fro!' I ordered. And she stopped. I sat on the piano stool. In a softer tone I said, 'It's not entirely your fault. You've imbibed too much of your father's sick theories and prurient curiosity. By the way, I saw him last week, getting off the train from Munich.'

'Yes, he's been to a conference there. With Frau Lou and some other colleagues.'

'He fainted on the platform.'

Her eyes grew larger still, from surprise. 'Really? He didn't tell us that. He wouldn't tell us; he'd be too proud. He has fainted before on occasions, in moments of emotional stress.' For a split-second, a bleak half-smile as she added, 'That's Jewish men for you, Wolf! Very female.'

'But what emotional stress was there in getting off a train?'

'Well, because he saw you. He did tell me he had seen you and he felt disturbed. He said it was like seeing his *Doppelgänger*. His double. It's more or less what he told you in that letter.'

I said I recalled it vaguely but hadn't really taken it in, being too angry at the rest. 'Perhaps you would care to remind me how he could resemble a penniless struggling artist and sometime railway porter?'

'You really don't remember? His family was quite poor too, struggling grain merchants. From a small town in Moravia not so far away from where your family came from. His father was old enough to be his grandfather, so he had much older half-brothers who went off elsewhere, just as I think you had, Wolf?'

'One half-brother,' I conceded.

'Most important, he had a young and beautiful mother whom he adored. Now my whining, smelly, yiddish-speaking grandma! His father had had two previous marriages, just like yours. The first two, in each case, involving a degree of confusion and uncertainty. You both had younger brothers who died. Don't you agree it's quite extraordinary?'

'But he's Jewish and I'm not.'

She flung her arm out as if this was trivial, saying, 'He assumed you were at first, and that impression has stayed with him. Anyway, he sees you as his double and it frightens him. You frightened him again, appearing so unexpectedly at the station. He's very superstitious, like, believing he will die in a certain year, I forget which. He said to me, "That young man is my death." Ludicrous!'

'Absolutely crazy.'

She nodded. 'He's also in an emotional state because his favourite disciple, a Dr Jung, is betraying him. He says he buried the hatchet with him in Munich, but should have buried it *in* him!' A twisted smile. 'Add to that, his precious "Sunday child" is going to be marrying and leaving us forever in two months. Max is visiting us now: horrid man, who takes every opportunity to grab my bottom in secret. Even while he's smiling and cooing at Sophie!'

I tapped out absent-mindedly on the piano a few bars of a love-duet in my never-to-be-finished opera. My tendons had been cut, at birth. Almost in counterpoint to the amorous chords she said, 'Papa may also be disturbed because he's in love with Frau Lou. That woman has already tortured Nietzsche and the poet Rilke, so why not my father too?' She twisted her body to plant her large feet on the floor, at last shrugged off her overcoat, stood up, and came across to me. She placed her hands on my shoulders. 'Please hold me for a moment, Wolf. I know you are very angry with me, but I'm feeling terribly sad, terribly unwell.'

'Yes,' I admitted, 'you look thin and poorly.' I laid my arms loosely around her. She laid her head against mine. 'Why are you sad, Anna dear?'

I could feel a tear touch my cheek. 'Thank you for that endearment. They're sending me away, to take the waters at Merano, for three months. For my health, they say! The warmer winter. I'm to stay with some friends, whom I dislike. I won't be able to see you, or even attend my own sister's wedding! Papa thinks I'm jealous of her, so it's best if I'm not here.' She ended savagely: 'I hate papa!'

'You don't, you love him. You adore him.'

'Not adore... I want to punish him, for hurting me. The last straw was sending me off with Eli to Switzerland instead of going walking with him and aunt Minna. I've thought of running away and not telling them where I am. Make them think I might have thrown myself in the Danube! In fact I think I *will* do that!' Now she was sobbing. I stood up and moved her back to the bed, and sat down beside her, holding her hand.

I said, almost playfully: 'What would punish him far worse, Anna, is if we were found here, lying on the bed naked together, dead, a revolver in my hand! You and his double!'

I felt her start to shiver; to shiver all through her body, as if she still had a fever. 'Oh yes!' she cried. 'Can we do that? That would be so good! Like Prince Rudolf and Mary Vetsera.'

'Yes.'

'Completely like them? I mean... before...'

'I think so, don't you? It would punish him even more if he knew you had been... defiled, and by me.'

Her body gave a final, comprehensive shudder. She squeezed my hand so tightly that it hurt. I tried to laugh the whole thing off, saying the only flaw in that idea was that we had no revolver. 'Oh, but I know where to get one, Wolf! My brother, Martin. He has one from his military training, and it's still in his room. It's in a drawer, under his underwear. I overheard him with a friend when he was on vacation from University. He was telling Hans not to wave it about, as it was loaded. Later, when he'd gone back to University, I found it.' She gripped my hands in both hers, and stared fiercely into my eyes. 'Can we do that?—Oh, but you want to live.'

'I'm not sure I do.' I looked around at the drab, dusty room; the smoky kerosene lamp; the grimy window that rarely let light in. There would be a certain grim pleasure in thinking of the grief, guilt and shame that would overcome the Freud family, so undeservedly prosperous, and so contemptuous of me. Sophie ignoring me at the station, as if I were less than a cockroach. Feeling adrift from reality, as if drunk, I heard myself saying, 'Think it over. Sleep on it. Come the day after tomorrow, at five, if you still feel the same way and have the gun... Now please go, I'm exhausted.'

'Alright.' She stood to put on and button her coat, put on her beret; stooped to kiss my cheek, then my mouth. As she was going out the door I called after her: 'And if you bring it, get hold of some money too. We'll have a lovely meal first.'

'I'll try, Wolf dear.'

When I heard the sound of the front door being shut, I threw myself on the bed. It was absurd. It wouldn't happen. Anyway, in the warmth of the Freud apartment, assailed by flavoursome smells from the kitchen, she would come to her senses very rapidly.

I noticed, on the small table where our lamp stood, a glimmer of white. A letter. I sprang up and went to get it. Official-looking. I tore it open. From the Art Academy. My heart beat more quickly with hope. No: 'We cannot offer... not enough faces in your pictures...' I threw it to the floor. Not enough faces! Jewish professors, surely—with no feeling for a beautiful landscape.

They would never let me escape from the Waldviertal, poverty, misery. Loneliness.

I hoped she would bring the revolver.

Feeling tearful, I lay down again. I had enough money to afford a simple meal, but I couldn't be bothered to go out. I lapsed into memories of brighter times. Like wandering through the woods around the Lichtenhag Ruins, with Gustl, sketching what I imagined the original castle to have looked like, with its pinnacles and turrets. Always my sketchbook with me, to draw the wonderful countryside. And Klara's face, so pure and lovely, and my mother's, translucent in her dying days... And Bruckner at St. Florian's. God's organist! Why had I come to this? Well, that was easy to answer: no helping hand! No money! No proper education!

No way out of this! And a gypsy within me, some spark of intuition, had told me I would die together with a woman. Not the gypsy who had foretold I would make famous buildings—in Poland, of all unlikely, dismal countries! And there would be no attachment to a woman called Geli, nor high-ranking officer called Paul who would betray me! Stupid. Best to trust one's own intuitions.

Dr Freud would find he could trust his. I smiled bleakly to myself. I would certainly be the death of him. If she brought the revolver. I hoped she would bring the revolver.

I woke some two hours later, not realising I had slept. The lamp had gone out. I had been whirled in a maelstrom, desperately trying to swim to a sunlit bank where my mother was holding out her arms to me imploringly. On another bank, murky, was a forest where wolves were howling. However hard I'd tried, the current seemed to be pulling me towards the wolves.

I lay, exhausted emotionally. Vaguely I recalled a dream that Gustl and I had made up for me to use with Dr Freud. It was so like this real one!

Hunger pangs cramped my stomach. I remembered Anna and our ridiculous talk. But then, was it so ridiculous? I had nothing to look forward to, and she... was too plain to find a husband and her aged parents would want her to look after them in their dotage.

Yet my mama... the memory of her holding out her arms imploringly was so strong still. It was the most vivid image of her I had had since her death. Dr Bloch... I'm afraid it's incurable... *Why* is it incurable? That just means you don't know how to cure it, you Jewish moron! You Jews are supposed to know everything!

I don't remember the rest of that evening and night, except that my mind was in a turbulent state.

23

I felt numb and distant from myself for most of the next day, staying in bed. However, though in a kind of waking dream, I still retained a sense of honour. A kindly dealer in the Leopoldstadt had invited me to sketch a small park, of little distinction, but for which one of his clients had a sentimental attachment: he had proposed to his wife there. I had made the sketch but not yet delivered it. The dealer had paid me in advance— a pitiful sum, but nonetheless I felt honour bound to deliver the picture.

That task is what led me, late in the evening, to the Berggasse area. A moonlit night, few people about. I was about to turn a corner when I was confronted close-up by Dr Freud heading homewards. He reeled back in shock. He croaked out my name: 'Herr Stiedler!'

'Yes. I hope you are not going to faint on seeing me, as you did at the railway station, Dr Freud!'

We had stopped in our tracks face to face. He stammered something incomprehensible, then grasped my arm. 'It's too cold to talk here,' he said, 'but come with me. Have you time for a glass of something? A nightcap?' He nodded in the direction of the nearby coffee house, the very one where I had read his confounded letter of dismissal.

'Yes.'

Still grasping my arm he moved me towards the café. 'I've escorted a female colleague back to her hotel,' he explained unnecessarily, as if he feared I suspected some immorality on his part.

The café was quiet, with just a few aged, yarmulka'd men hunched over newspapers or books as they sipped coffee. We were soon drinking and I was breathing in the noxious fumes of his cigar. He wanted to know why I knew about his fainting fit and pretended to be surprised that I had been present at the scene. He believed, he said dishonestly, that he had been assailed by overwhelming, enfeebling grief at returning to a city he loved but had lost. Lost, he explained, because it had fallen into the hands of Mayor Lueger and Schönerer and their anti-Semitic rabble. Jews had practically created Vienna's high culture in the past twenty years, and this was the thanks they got! The anti-Semites had overthrown reason, culture, enlightenment—all that had made life worth living in Vienna, and to which the Jews had made an incalculable contri-bution. All that was left was hedonism, operettas and the *heuringer*. And so on. I of course nodded and shrugged as seemed appropriate.

He asked how I had been doing; said I looked pale and thin; then that he was glad we had met because his conscience was somewhat troubled over me. 'You did lie to me, Wolf, but I should expect that from a patient and I realise I was partly to blame. I wanted you to be Jewish. I don't quite know why. I thought you *must* be Jewish because you possessed energy, passion and ideas. I really do think you could become a successful, innovative town planner. You have a very Jewish family loyalty, as you showed in your loving care for your sick mother.' He leaned forward and peered intently into my eyes as he went on: 'I would guess you also have a considerable capacity for hate, which can be a virtue; I possess it too! In my letter to you I told you the truth, but not the whole truth. The fact is, you had made a considerable impression on my daughter Anna.' He smiled apologetically. 'Not your fault. I'm sure you did nothing to encourage it.'

'Absolutely nothing. You astonish me.'

'She is at an impressionable age. She had helped you, and that, I think, made her believe she could be your saviour. Females are like that.'

'She was very kind. How is she?'

He frowned, sighed. 'She has not been well. We're packing her off to stay with friends in Merano for the winter, hoping the better cli-mate will do her good.'

'Give her my regards.'

'I will.'

I was sure he would not.

'Even apart from her youth,' he continued, 'I don't believe she is cut out for marriage and motherhood.'

He had said what he wanted to say and looked at his watch. 'They will wonder where I am.' He summoned a waiter for the bill and, while paying for our drinks, pressed me to accept some notes. 'For some steak dinners.' I declined them, saying he had already been too kind.

We parted civilly, with a handshake. I enjoyed the thought that within twenty four hours he would find himself grief-stricken, and would recall this encounter with horror. *If* she came. The odds were heavily against it. She was so young, and in her comfortable family atmosphere she would surely think a winter at a delightful resort much preferable to extinction. *I* would have settled for Merano, in a no doubt friendly home with plentiful food, warmth and leisure.

I delivered my picture. The twinkly-eyed Shylock, at work still with his ledgers, gazed at it then at me over his spectacles. 'Not bad, not bad at all, young man. I think my client will be pleased. That little marble Cupid, and the fountain, you've done those not at all badly.'

24

It was well past the appointed hour and she had not come. It was not a surprise, but I felt disappointed and frustrated. I wondered what to do with myself. Perhaps I would go into the centre, join some noisy Communist or nationalist demonstration, get in a few strong punches to kidneys, always melting away swiftly. I had done this a few times; it could be amusing to watch the mayhem, the internecine fighting, this could induce.

Then I heard the rapid patter of her footsteps coming up the stairs, and my heart fluttered. She rushed into the room, a small suitcase in her hand, breathing heavily, a hectic flush in her cheeks. She dropped the suitcase, moved straight into my arms and kissed me on the lips. 'I'm sorry I'm late; I had to go a long way round to avoid a march.' I could hear phlegm rasping in her chest. I drew back, fearing to be infected— illogical though that was!—saying, 'You're really still not well.'

'What does that matter? I shall be well enough soon, my dear.' She fumbled in the inner pocket of her coat. 'I've brought lots of money. I asked papa if I could have some to buy clothes for Merano. He was surprised, as I don't usually bother about clothes. Here.' She pressed a thick wad of banknotes into my hand. She crouched to open her case, then reached her hand in. 'And here—is what we want.' She brought to light a quite magnificent weapon. I couldn't help gasping at its heaviness and glitter as I took it into my hands.

'It's an Austrian army Gasser!' I said, turning it over. 'Anna, this is an amazing weapon!... It takes five bullets... And are they live?'

She nodded, her eyes sparkling almost merrily. 'Yes, I heard Martin warn his friend they were live, so to stop waving it about.'

'Superb!' I kept turning the weighty revolver over in my hands, in awe. I could see it was well-used, but in good condition. Had it killed any men? How many? So much potential for death.

'Let's get ready to go out, Wolf,' she said. 'We have all night—it seems an endless time. I told mama I was going to meet a friend and then go to the theatre with her, to explain why I'm dressed up; as dressed up as I can be.' She grimaced. 'And said I would probably stay the night with her. I'm quite hungry. We can afford a nice restaurant; well, not too high-class, of course, as my dress is very ordinary.' She unbuttoned her coat so I could see her dress, looking at me with a shy, anxious expression.

'It's lovely. You could walk straight into the Hotel Sacher and people would stare in admiration; but'—I chuckled—'I'm not exactly…' I didn't need to finish. She crouched over her case again, saying she had brought one of Martin's waistcoats and a bow tie which she thought might look nice on me. And she had brought a pair of scissors. I sat on the piano stool while she snipped away at my beard and hair to make me a little more presentable. As she leaned against me to snip a recalcitrant lock, I said her body felt different. 'I'm squeezed into a corset,' she explained; '—careful, I don't want to cut off your ear!… Normally I like to feel free, but I thought how tightly corseted Mary was, so I wanted to make an effort. Of course it's hopeless.' She sighed. 'I can never have a narrow waist, whatever I wear… There, you look much better.'

She suddenly broke into a long girlish giggle. I asked her what was funny. 'I suddenly saw mama and my aunt in this room, carefully dressing me, and then my brothers Ernst and Martin marching me out between them, as happened to Mary! And my stiff corset helping to keep me upright and as if alive! Then papa announcing I had died of pneumonia at home! Don't you think that would be hilarious?'

'Hilarious, yes.' I excused myself to visit the repulsive toilet along the corridor. When I returned I saw she was glancing through the leather-bound *Crime and Punishment.* 'A beautiful edition,' she said. 'How did you come by it? I see it was a gift to Frau Eckstein. The banker's wife?'

'Yes. It was in their library.'

Puzzled, she said, 'Did she lend it to you?'

'No, I stole it.'

'You stole it!' She gave a shocked laugh.

'They have so much and I so little.'

'I suppose you're right.'

'Some of the pages were uncut. She would never have read it, it's far too intellectual for the female mind. Anyway, it will be found, when they find us, and returned to her.'

An hour later we were in a restaurant just off the Ringstrasse, seated at a table near a blazing fire. I had never been in such a restaurant. It was well known as a hot-bed of anti-Semitism; Anna had suggested it since there was no chance of finding Jews who might recognise her there. A candelabra shimmered overhead. Rich red walls. Opulence. We had attracted some curious and disapproving glances from waiters and diners as we had entered. I assumed because of my still-scruffy appearance, or Anna's slightly Jewish features, or probably both.

A waiter brought a bottle of wine in a bucket of ice, and poured a dribble into my glass. I waited for him to fill the glass, but he stayed frozen. Anna said, 'Drink it to see if it's alright.' I did so, and nodded, feeling a mixture of shame at my 'ignorance' and contempt for such absurd bourgeois habits. If one orders a strudel, the waiter does not extract a spoonful and feed it into one's mouth for you to pronounce it satisfactory. Neither of us drank more than a glass of wine.

Over our food, she began to talk in a nervously cheerful, brittle manner. She wondered how many of the couples around us, who were observing us with distaste, were actually in a clandestine relationship. Most of them, if one could judge by the stories of Arthur Schnitzler! He had been to their apartment for supper, and she had noticed his eyes mentally undress Sophie. A charming rogue. She and Sophie would sometimes wonder if this or that friend's mother was the dissolute, unfaithful woman in Herr Schnitzler's latest. They would see her, in their minds, reclining on the wrong bed with the wrong man, when in all probability the poor woman was leading an entirely blameless, if tedious, life. Sophie, whose mind was very literal, might observe that Frau X could not be that easily seduced heroine because she had three children not two, and her hair was black, not blond; and Anna would respond that that was stupid, since fiction writers change details, in order to avoid being accused of libel. So this character's having three children, and black hair, made it the more likely that she was Frau X!

And so on and so on. I would nod politely, and occasionally smile, while feeling weirdly separate from my surroundings, my loquacious companion, and even myself. We took a glass of cognac during the dessert stage. I wasn't used to mixing alcoholic drinks, or indeed to any alcohol. I could hear a ringing in my ears. She was saying she could see I was bored, and I wrenched myself back with a great effort: 'No, not at all.'

'It feels very strange,' she said, 'to be talking about these normal things—well, normal in some circles—when we know what's going to happen.' Putting her fork down decisively on her plate of scarcely-touched exotic fruits and ice creams, she turned her gaze towards the fire. 'Whenever I've thought of Prince Rudolf and Mary,' she went on, 'I've imagined the blazing fire in their room. The snow pelting against the big windows, but they are warm, in their own world, drinking champagne... And gradually the fire dying down, turning to coals, then ash... I'm feeling very nervous, Wolf dear.'

'That's natural.'

'I wonder will it hurt.'

'I imagine it's instantaneous, there's no pain.'

'But I don't suppose you know either—whether it hurts.'

'Well—no,' I said, puzzled.

With a faraway look: 'But then, it *ought* to hurt. It's such a momentous event.'

'Anna, we don't have to do it, you know.'

'Oh, but I want to. Even though the thought makes me shiver. Do *you* want to?'

'Yes.'

'I'm so glad!' She slid her fingers between mine, and lifted both our hands from the table, as if taking a vow. 'So I shall know, just once in my short life, what Frau Lou meant.'

I frowned in puzzlement. 'What she meant?'

'By the reception of the semen being the height of ecstasy. She talks to papa about it. Often! I... overhear sometimes.' She had the grace to blush. 'She wants it all the time, she says, wherever she is, wherever there is a man, whatever she is doing. She might be playing bridge, or swimming in the sea, she craves that ecstatic experience. Papa of course just listens and grunts. And perhaps wishes it were he giving her that ecstasy. Well, I shall have that experience. Once. But of course it's scary.'

I realised I had been misunderstanding her, but managed to keep it from showing in my face. This girl was more worried about something stupid and trivial like, to put it grossly, a fuck than about dying! She hurried on after a sip of coffee, her eyes glittering feverishly: 'I've kept trying to imagine that ecstasy. I assume there is a moment when, for the girl, a half-hearted or even unwilling response turns into—something more, something I can't begin to imagine: a rapture. When even if your father burst in on you, you simply couldn't stop. You'd cry out, "Papa, I'm sorry, but you'll have to wait; I can't stop this... Your theories about it never told me of this divine sensation..." And papa would just stand in the doorway, rooted to the spot, his mouth gaping!' And Anna threw her head back and laughed. She quelled it, turned it into a wry smile, lowering her gaze. 'Or perhaps he'd say, "I understand. I forgive you."' She lifted her napkin to her face, and I saw a glint of tears. She sniffed, smiled brightly again, and picked up her cognac glass.

'You haven't eaten your dessert.'

'I couldn't; I would burst in this corset. My first adult corset and my first cognac! Before my first...' She left it unsaid. 'Papa hates girls being tight-laced, so I suppose this too is a slight rebellion.'

'Waste not want not,' I said, taking her plate. As the partly melted ice cream slid deliciously down my throat I reflected that this was the last food I would taste. The last supper. It seemed unreal. I supposed because, despite my manifold deprivations, I felt reasonably healthy. Condemned felons must feel the same.

I tipped our waiter generously, with a feeling of rare munificence, thanks to the good Dr Freud. On our walk back to the lodgings we confronted suddenly, turning a corner, a rowdy march. Czechs, Slovaks, Magyars, Ruthenians, who knows who they were, believing that happiness lay just around *their* corner, if only they could be released from old Franz Josef and his tyranny. I let go of Anna's hand and infiltrated into the march, shouting inane, meaningless slogans which no one could hear, for all the hubbub. Then I kicked the man in front of me hard in the shins; he bellowed, but before he could find out who had kicked him I had melted away and, clutching Anna's hand again, as though we were lovers with no interest in politics, or anything but romance, walked quickly on, away from them, towards the darkness and silence.

25

We lay side by side, naked. Our room, chilly, sombre, and pervaded by the foul kerosene smell, seemed far from the palatial hunting lodge at Mayerling. On our return from the restaurant she had taken three letters from her suitcase, and placed them on the small table, explaining that they were to her father, mother and Sophie, all addressed to her home so that there would be no delay in finding out who she was. We had undressed shyly, our backs turned to each other. It felt odd that I had no need to place my trousers under the mattress to get a crease. Once in bed we had hugged for warmth, and kissed.

I felt no desire. I stared at the ceiling while she described what she had written to her parents. How she felt useless, and had never been wanted by them, a mere unfortunate late accident. She was the Cinderella of the sisters, and this was best for everyone. They were not to blame themselves. She thanked them for everything. She was sorry she had had to deceive them over continuing to meet me.

We kissed again, and touched. I felt no desire. The Gasser revolver lay on the floor on my side of the bed. We touched some more. Still there was no desire. She whispered to me, 'I'm sorry. I have no experience, you see.'

'No, I'm sorry. Why don't you go into your fantasy?'

'Shall I? You don't mind? The Prince and the Soldier, just once more...'

She moved apart from me. I leaned up on my elbow and looked down at her face. I saw her teeth clench and all the muscles and nerves in her face tighten. She made an occasional grunting or gasping sound. Her whole body was rigid; she might have been in the agonising grip of lockjaw. I felt her unbearable tension affect me, jangling my nerves. I tried to 'hear' Gustl playing the slow movement of Beethoven's 'Moonlight,' but it didn't work.

Suddenly she gave a loud groan and twisted around on her front. 'Beat me, Wolf! Beat me! A child is being beaten! A child is being beaten!' I looked around for something to beat her with. I wanted to beat her, to ease my screaming nerves. I got out of bed and picked up her corset lying on the chair. Lighter than my mother's, when I had reverently packed both of hers away in a box, with all her other underclothes and night-clothes, that dreadful Christmas Eve. Different also in that this one had the new stocking suspenders hanging down from the front. I had seen these before only on the corrupt body of a whore, in Anna's company, and in a prurient shop window display I had hurried past; and these sordid memories added to the savage pleasure of kneeling over her, the rolled-up corset in my hand, the long straps, with heavy buckles at the end, acting like a cat o' nine tails. I called out the number of each blow: '...five... six... seven...' Jew-whore, I thought. She was moaning, the metal hooks biting into her buttocks, leaving red weals. 'Thirteen... fourteen... fifteen...' I felt no desire, no lust. Anger only. At her, at my father, at the stupid Art academicians, at everyone.

A shudder went through her, and she twisted round on to her back, panting. Ashamed of myself and her, I threw the loathsome garment, created to arouse lust in both wearer and watcher, across the room. There were tears visible on her cheeks, yet she was smiling. She murmured, her eyes closed and dreamy, 'Now you must say, I forgive you, dear friend.' I muttered the words. She pulled me down beside her and covered my face in kisses, smearing it with her tears. After a few moments I pulled my face away, lay straight, gazing up at the ceiling again. Gradually her panting faded away, till we lay in a silence broken only by her occasional coughing.

I drifted into a drowse, in which Gustl and I were standing in Bruckner's humble room at St Florian. I was roused by the sound of sobbing. Anna was sitting up in bed, her arms hiding her breasts, her face buried in her hands. I asked her, sleepily, what was wrong.

She lowered her hands and gazed down at me. She looked suddenly quite ancient, a desolate crone, like Donatello's Magdalene, in the dim light. 'It's no good, Wolf,' she said in a hopeless tone. 'I'm bad. After the relief and the forgiveness, there's this great remorse, because I can never be punished enough for my sin.'

'What sin?'

She waited some moments before replying. 'It's hard for me to say it. I need to be beaten because I love my father. Too much. I can never love anyone else. He is the Prince and I am his Soldier. It was foolish to think I could sleep with you. It's always him I imagine beating me, to punish me for what I want with him, which is too much. How *could* you feel aroused? It wasn't your fault, my dear.'

I could scarcely believe what I had heard. I lay like a stone. She was absently stroking my thigh. At last she said in weary tones, 'I can't expect you to understand: how could anyone? Only papa. I've told him, while lying on the couch, and he understands. Of course.'

'Oh, of course!'

'But his understanding doesn't cure me of my guilt, my self-hatred. And sometimes I project that outwards, so that I hate everybody— mama, papa, Sophie, people who push past me in the street, Germans, Czechs, Jews—everybody. Then I feel even more wicked. I think we probably have that in common, that projection outwards. It may be the only point where we meet... So, really, the only answer is—Martin's revolver. I'm ready.'

I said, icily, slowly: 'Let me get this clear: you want to be fucked by your father?'

'No—no—well...' There was a long pause. 'Oh God, it was much easier explaining *you*. Or trying to. In my case it's much more complicated than... what you said. I want his baby, certainly. I would never want the sexual act with him in reality, it would be unimaginable, unconscionable, but...' She continued, mumbling incoherently: but if one got rid of all the pretentious rigmarole, the answer clearly was: Yes.

An image of my saintly mother floated before my eyes. The thought of having any such grotesque desires for her was nauseating. I said, 'Your father may understand you, but I certainly don't.' I got out of bed and slipped hurriedly into my trousers and shirt. Then I spoke, in my coldest voice, staring at the black window, since I felt too much disgust to look at her. 'I recall what he insultingly said to me in that letter, Anna—that I was afloat on a river, and it was up to me which bank I landed on, the dark side or the light side. I need no lessons in morality from your depraved and corrupting father. But I'm going to say to you now, you're in great danger of landing on the dark side—even if you have not already landed there. On this side, a decent, moral life, presumably as a spinster, for obvious reasons; on that side, degradation, corruption, damnation. It's your choice.' I heard her whimpering faintly, then whisper something inaudible.

'What did you say?'

A slightly louder whisper: 'I said I know I am bad, very bad.'

'You are very sick, very sick in the head. You and your father thought that *I* was sick; but it is you. Probably it's something to do with being Jewish; a sick sexual obsession. I've heard it before of Jewish females, and you've shown it to me before—but I didn't know it could go this far. Now get dressed, please. I want nothing more to do with you. Take your brother's revolver with you. Thank God I've been spared from dying with such a creature. And even more from fucking you, since it wouldn't surprise me if you are carrying a sexual disease. The reason I was not able to is that you are more male than female— which you twisted into that gross so-called theory about me.'

She did not stir; but said in a timid voice: 'Oh, this is truly a punishment. Only now you should say, "I forgive you, dear friend! I forgive you your indecent, incestuous wishes."'

'Get out of my room!'

She leapt off the bed like a frightened animal and started scrabbling blindly for her clothes. I picked up the Gasser and emptied the bullets out onto the floor. There were three. It would have been enough, and more. I knew better than to risk having this sick Jew girl shoot herself and so be on my conscience.

She dressed quickly and incompletely; stowed revolver, corset, waistcoat, bow tie, scissors and the suicide letters into the suitcase. An almost inaudible 'Goodbye' at the door, and she was gone. Out of my life. I breathed in deeply, in sheer relief; then sat at the piano and hammered out some clumsy, amateurish chords. Life, I thought! Life!

26

I decided that night that I'd had enough of the syphilitic whore, Vienna. Besides, I had led a charmed life in avoiding the call-up, but my luck couldn't hold forever.

I slept like a baby, and when I woke late, with the daylight already sneaking through the grimy window, I felt fresh. I lay for a long time, my arm behind my head, slowly turning over the events of a few hours ago: addressing myself silently. Also with the spectre of Gustl on the piano stool, listening and nodding...

'How amazing! And how unfair life is! Here I am, by no means perfect, with normal human faults, but for all that a decent young man, with huge talents... And there is she, granted all the blessings of a cultured, well-to-do home and a fine education, yet her mind, thanks to her father and her race, is a seething swamp...' Then, in sheer relief, I cried aloud 'Ouf!', as if expressing disgust while sweeping some cockroach or spider off my body.

Would I, I wondered, have gone through with the execution and suicide? I really didn't know. Probably not; probably I had not reached the ultimate despair of such an act. But, whether or not, I now thanked God that I had come to my senses. Nor had I made the fatal mistake of physical intimacy with her. Something in me, or above me, had allowed me to preserve my decency, sanity and health. It was bad enough that she had kissed me on the mouth; but I could tolerate a respiratory infection.

I still had about half the sum that Anna had given me to pay for our meal. I felt a slight pang of conscience, wondering if I should return it to her. But how? It seemed best to regard this money as a small restitution for having been forced into the lower depths.

I spent the next two days in writing, catching up with events in this —I suppose I must call it—memoir. *1912 Overture* no longer seemed adequate as a title; it did not express the moral danger I had been in. There would be time aplenty to find a title more fitting.

Then I packed up my few possessions. Besides this notebook I packed only the Dostoievsky: not wanting a stolen book to be found here. I might be able to sell it somewhere far from Vienna. It was All Souls' Day when I set off for the station. The trams were packed with people carrying picnic baskets, heading for the Central Cemetery where they would pass the day with their dead. And after dark the cemetery would be ablaze with candles. I had gone one year, to do some sketches. Today, in murky wintry light, the faces peering out from the trams appeared to be dead themselves, cadaverous, sepulchral, ghostly. A great many of the younger men would be dead in reality very soon, I felt, in the coming conflagration, and I rejoiced in that idea.

I took a train to Linz. There I wandered the familiar streets, and laid flowers on my mother's grave, weeping as I did so. How much sweeter and more Germanic was this town, set in the green countryside, than Vienna! Its folk more down to earth, speaking just the one proper language, and even the Danube more clear and sparkling.

As I walked through busy streets I saw a figure I recognised coming towards me. I felt my cheeks burning, fixed my eyes on the road, and strode quickly by. But a voice from behind me: 'Young Herr Hitler, isn't it?' I stopped, turned and, affecting surprise, said, 'Ah, Dr Bloch!' Grey beard, black coat and hat, black doctors' bag. He looked older, stooped, worn down; but his eyes twinkled as he shook my hand warmly. 'How are you, Adolf?'

'Well, sir.'

'That's good. Visiting your sister?'

'Yes.'

'How's your life in Vienna?' His eyes seemed to be examining mine shrewdly.

'Oh, good. My pictures are selling well.'

'That's splendid! Your mother, you know, worried how you'd cope with her... gone. Dear woman. I told her I thought you'd be fine.'

'I am, sir.'

Saying he had to be off to see to a patient, he shook my hand again and walked on. No mention of his encounter with Freud. Keeping confidence. And perhaps not wanting to embarrass me. I couldn't think unkindly of him. My legs trembled though, as I resumed my stroll. Seeing him brought back all that pain.

I spent two days and nights with my half-sister. Our couple of hours in the Prater had eased us back into some of our old familiarity as children; indeed, both now being mature, we got on much better than we had done then. I dandled little Geli, my niece, on my lap, and sketched her. She truly is a charming little girl, with large, lustrous, appealing eyes. I loved the way, when I gave her a piggy-back, her little arms clung around my neck and she murmured sweetly in my ear, 'Thank you, Uncle Adi'. I could see for myself what a hard time my sister had, and I swore to myself that if I were ever in a position to be able to do so I would have them both come and live with me.

I paid a courtesy visit to Gustl's mother, and at her insistence stayed for a meal with her and her husband. Since I had once saved her from drowning, the plump, homely woman regards me as a knight in shining armour. Topics of conversation over the supper table: Gustl (fit and well, the last they'd heard of him, training somewhere in the east), my ideas about beautifying Linz, the sports club, the women's guild, church festivals and charities, and their small upholstery business, which they had hoped Gustl would take over. But if music was to be his career, so be it. Good, kind people, speaking in their soft Austrian-German dia-lect: salt of the earth. Their minds are not cesspools, as the theories of Freud and his kind imagine, simply because their own minds are made that way, but straightforward, simple and decent. We had one minor dis-agreement. I had been describing the scum and riff-raff polluting Vienna. Mrs Kubelik said to me, 'We are all God's children, my dear. "Judge not that ye be not judged".' Her husband nodded in agreement. I felt stung by the rebuke, and was on the point of snapping back; but with great self-control I stifled the impulse, simply responding, 'You are true Christians.' They are elderly, and have been fed from childhood the stupid doctrine of love and compassion for all, as preached by the church. There was no point disturbing them at their age with home truths, and we parted on warm terms.

Then I struck out, by train and ox-cart, into the bleak Waldviertel, where I walked around and slept in barns and under hedges. Despite carrying a pack, grown heavier from food supplies from Gustl's mother, I felt relieved of a great burden. I had had my blood sucked out of me by those vampires in Vienna, but now, as I breathed the fresh country air, my red blood cells were increasing, strengthening, coursing through my body.

I passed through Dollersheim, the village of my ancestors. Nothing stirred there, except for some listless, scrawny hens and cats, a mangy dog, and a few slack-jawed, steep-browed peasants, the result of centuries of inbreeding. It seemed to me that the nondescript, mournful village should be wiped from the face of the earth. I went to the town of Graz, where my father's mother, Maria Schikelgruber, had been employed by, supposedly, a Jew called Frankenberger. I questioned several very old people, and no one could remember a rich family of that name. Nor indeed could they remember a Schikelgruber. So much for ancestral family legends! And so much for the 'Nightmare'. That engraving in the Freud apartment came back to me one night, in a barn; only it was not a beautiful, helpless maiden lying under the leering, hook-nosed incubus but I myself. I awoke from it crying out and bathed in sweat. Whether or not my grandmother was seduced by a Jewish master, I felt it should be a crime for Jews to employ female domestics of childbearing age.

I moved on to Braunau am Inn where I'd been born. I wandered around the quiet border town, reflecting on the coincidence of my birth, occurring almost at the same time as the death of the last, frail hope of the doomed old world, Crown Prince Rudolf. I found a barber's shop, and had my beard shaved off and my hair and moustache trimmed.

The first snow of the winter fell, but only left me feeling more exhilarated and hopeful; and I earned a crust by clearing the drifts outside some grand riverside houses. I stood on the bridge for some time, leaning on its stone wall and gazing at the water below, then I crossed into Germany.

8 April 1981

Dr B. Fischer,
73 rue Cavendish,
Zurich

Dear Bernhardt,

Thank you with all my heart for your magnanimous gesture in purchasing the so-called memoir and passing it straight to me. Whether a forgery or genuine (but full of lies), it must have cost you an outrageous sum. I am only glad that this 'Herr Meyer' chose to offer it to you, my dear friend, rather than any other dealer in rare manuscripts. I could call his choice divine grace if I believed in a divinity. I know you have done me this great service purely out of love for my father and me.

I yield totally to your expertise when you say the handwriting and syntax appear prima facie authentic, or at least persuasive. I can confirm that this type of notebook was commonly on sale in Vienna at that time; I possessed one myself. Now, the story of how this particular one came into Herr Meyer's hands... I suppose it is just credible that a small Bavarian boy could have hidden it (and Frau Eckstein's Dostoievsky) as a prank against the 'nice, quiet tenant', then found he had quit Munich in a rush to join the fight for the Fatherland; told his parents it had been a gift and kept it all these years. Now, old, wishes to leave his grandchildren something, and no longer fears to reveal its existence. It is, yes, just believable. Though unlikely.

I read it of course with a mixture of distaste and horror. The apparent predictions, like the sad fate of our poor Sophie, the 'bath-house', von Paulus ('Paul') 'betraying' Hitler by surrendering at Stalingrad, etc., argue strongly for a much more recent date of composition. As for my early fantasy life, the child being beaten, and so on, it has been much written about in the analytic literature, as you know. Grossly distorted by this 'author', needless to say. Distorted so as to imply that he and 'Anna' were mirror-images of each other. Cut from the same cloth! Only distinguished one from the other by my having everything and he nothing. Leaving aside entirely the question of character!

One knows that he suffered temporary blindness during the First World War, but one has never heard of this happening to him in earlier years. I am sure papa never treated him; just as papa never lectured or wrote about Donatello. Leonardo and Michelangelo yes, of course, but never Donatello. His knowledge of our family *circumstances is very limited, for instance, where are Oliver and Ernst? There are numerous factual errors regarding that period of our life at 19 Berggasse.*

Is any of it true? It's true that acquaintances of the young Hitler have written that he looked quite Jewish at times, and had 'big desert-walking feet'. I am old, and my memory of almost seventy years ago very clouded. The only incident which does echo disturbingly is of attending a lecture by Karl May with my sister and afterwards having coffee with a polite but scruffy young man who looked like a Jew from the east. Perhaps, whoever he was, he was a total fantasist who knew we were the notorious Freud's daughters, and from that created his scurrilous make-believe world.

I may even have attended a symphony concert with him. I can't be sure. So much has happened since then (my God!), and so much is lost 'in the dark backward and abysm of time'. Pseudo-memories can too readily occur to one when reading such a narrative, and I have experienced that troubling phenomenon during the past week. I even imagined I had read a few pages of it before, so deceitful one's mind can be.

I was certainly disturbed around the time of Sophie's wedding, and decadent Vienna encouraged morbid thoughts and fantasies (and suicides); but I think I would remember a suicide pact in a slum room with such an unsavoury young man, do you not agree?!

I am perplexed and troubled. I have to admit to myself that this fantasy 'Anna' is not unlike me at the time, as regards my psyche not my behaviour. I was a 'hunter in the snow', as the real young AH must have been. I hunted for selfhood, he for apocalypse.

My warmest thanks again. My love to dear Mathilde also and I hope to see you both when you next visit these islands. I am rather lonely. I still miss Dorothy dreadfully. I wear her sweaters around the house, and stroke them. It is some comfort.

Affectionately yours,

Anna Freud

Further Titles

All Cornwall Thunders at My Door: A Biography of Charles Causley
By Laurence Green

All Cornwall Thunders at My Door is the first full biography of Charles Causley to be published, timed to coincide with the 10th anniversary of his death in 2003. Laurence Green has compiled a great deal of information concerning Causley's life in Cornwall and beyond, of his personal history, his influences and motivations, helping to give context to the great legacy left to us by "the greatest poet laureate we never had."

"This is the first biography of Charles Causley, and takes us towards the heart of a marvellous poet and deeply intriguing man. It's all well done: clear, sympathetic, appreciative and shrewd. Everyone who loves Causley's poems will want to read it." — *Sir Andrew Motion*

Includes photographs not previously published and a foreword by Dr Alan M. Kent. Paperback, 220 pages. ISBN 978 1 908878 08 3.

Following 'An Gof': Leonard Truran, Cornish Activist and Publisher
By Derek R. Williams

Len Truran was, until his death in 1997, a highly influential figure within the fields of politics and culture in Cornwall. He joined Mebyon Kernow in 1964 and, over the years, acted as both secretary and chairman of the party. His publications, under the imprint of Dyllansow Truran, are widely recognised as being seminal in the story of Cornish publishing.

In this book Derek R. Williams explores the life of Len Truran, from his childhood through to his pivotal role in Mebyon Kernow and the campaign for the creation of a Cornish Assembly and on to the remarkably prolific and influential publisher he became.

Paperback, 104 pages. ISBN 978 1 908878 11 3.

The Fifties Mystique
By Jessica Mann

Many young women 'long to put the clock back to the post-war years when life seemed prettier and nicer.' In this book Jessica Mann demolishes such preconceptions about their mothers' or grandmothers' young days, showing that in reality life was uglier and nastier.

Born just before WW2, she grew up in the post-war era of austerity, restrictions and hypocrisy, before anyone even dreamed of Women's Lib. The Fifties Mystique is both a personal memoir and a polemic. In explaining the lives of pre-feminists to the post-feminists of today, Mann discusses the period's very different attitudes to sex, childbirth, motherhood and work, describes how she and other young women lived in that distant world with its forgotten restrictions and warns against taking hard-won rights for granted.

Jessica Mann is the author of 21 crime novels and 4 non-fiction books. As a journalist she has written for national newspapers, weeklies and glossy magazines and is the crime fiction critic of The Literary Review.

'Jessica Mann analyses the decade with forensic precision – stripping away the rose-coloured specs for good' — *The Daily Mail*

'thoughtful and emphatic ... a richly readable and persuasive piece of work' — *Penelope Lively, The Spectator*

an 'excellently readable book' — *Katharine Whitehorn*

'Her battle cry is full of vivid descriptions of the grim, snobbery and casual misogyny of postwar Britain. A crime-writer by trade, her barely veiled exasperation only makes the polemic more enjoyable ... ' — *The Mail on Sunday*

'an extremely engaging read: revealing, touching, informative and occasionally comic.' — *Simon Parker, The Western Morning News*

'She recalls the grime of the 50s: endless stinking nappy buckets; smog; inadequate washing facilities; body odour whenever people were crowded together. She recalls boredom and isolation, and suspects both the child-rearing experts and the government of a concerted push to get mothers back home after the war, so that there would be jobs for the returning 'boys'. And she recalls the unacceptability of talking, or sometimes even knowing, about sex, female anatomy, and cancer. She is bang on' — *Baroness Neuberger, The Jewish Chronicle*

Paperback, 224 pages. ISBN 978 1 908878 07 6.
First published by Quartet Books in 2012.

Gathering the Fragments: The Selected Essays of a Groundbreaking Historian
By Charles Thomas

This selection of work by Professor Charles Thomas, Cornwall's leading historian, focuses on the more elusive titles from his long and illustrious career and covers the whole range of his output from folklore and archaeology to military and local history, and from cerealogy to cryptozoology. The book also includes unpublished material, as well as specially composed introductions to each chapter, a full biography and a select bibliography.

Chapters featured include: A Plea for Neutrality (New Cornwall, 1955); Youthful Ventures Into the Realm of Folk Studies - Present-day Charmers in Cornwall (Folk-Lore, 1953), Underground Tunnels at Island Mahee, County Down (Ulster Folklife, 1957), Archaeology and Folk-life Studies (Gwerin, 1960); What Did They Do When it Rained in 1857? (The Scillonian, 1986); Home Thoughts from Abroad (Camborne Wesley Journal, 1948); The Day That Never Came (The Cornish Review, 1968); Camborne Festival Magazine - The Camborne Printing and Stationery Company (1971), The Camborne Students' Association (1974), Camborne's War Record, 1914-1919 (1976), The Camborne Volunteer Training Corps in World War One (1983), Carwynnen Quoit (1985); Jottings from Gwithian (The Godrevy Light) - How Far Back Can We Go? (2006), Ladies of Gwithian (2007); Two Funeral Orations (unpublished) - Charles Woolf (1984), Rudolf Glossop (1993); Archaeology and the Mind (unpublished) (1968 inaugural lecture, University of Leicester); The Archaeologist in Fiction (1976); Archaeology, and the Concept of Cornishness (unpublished) (1995 memorial lecture, Cornwall Archaeological Society); A Couple of Reviews - Lost Innocence: Archaeologists as People (Encounter, 1981), The Cairo Trilogy (Literary Review, 2001); An Impromptu Ode - To A.L. Rowse (1997); The Cerealogist - An Archaeologist's View (1991), Magnetic Anomalies (1991/92); Two Cryptozoological Papers - The "Monster" Episode in Adomnan's Life of St. Columba (Cryptozoology, 1988), A Black Cat Among the Pictish Beasts? (Pictish Arts Society Journal, 1994).

Professor Charles Thomas CBE DL DLitt FBA FSA is a former President of the Council for British Archaeology, the Society for Medieval Archaeology, the Royal Institution of Cornwall, the Cornwall Archaeological Society and the Cornish Methodist Historical Society. He is currently the President of The John Harris Society.

Edited by Chris Bond. Hardcover: ISBN 9781908878021. Paperback: ISBN 9781908878038. 216 pages.

Shut away! My early days fishing out of Newquay
By Rod Lyon

Rod Lyon, former Grand Bard of the Gorseth Kernow, recollects his early days fishing out of Newquay, "in the days before modern electronic aids, man-made fibre ropes, twines and cords, plastic 'skins' and floats instead of cork ... when navigation to and from the gear was by dead reckoning, using only a watch and a compass, with only experience telling you what to allow for with the tide." Rod illustrates, in both words and pictures, the techniques and the equipment used in those bygone days, and along the way remembers some of the more notable characters, both Cornish and Breton, who frequented 'down Quay'. The book also includes a gazetteer of his favourite fishing grounds.

Paperback, 120 pages. ISBN 978 1 908878 01 4.

Historical Descriptions of Camborne
Edited by Chris Bond

A fine selection of historical descriptions of the town and parish of Camborne spanning the years 1700 to 1898, including accounts of the parish by Edward Lhuyd, William Penaluna and Joseph Polsue. Also includes Richard Trevithick by Richard Edmonds, the elusive Reminiscences of Camborne by William Richards Tuck (which includes a first hand account of Joseph Emidy, the 18th century West African born slave turned composer and virtuoso violinist), Rodolph Eric Raspe, the author of the Adventures of Baron Munchausen, by Robert Hunt, The Endowed Public Charities of Camborne by Thomas Fiddick junior and The Great Dolcoath by Albert Bluett, this last being illustrated with photographs by J C Burrow of Camborne.

The book also contains a comprehensive index. All of the proceeds from the sales of this book are to go to the Camborne Old Cornwall Society, and the President of which, David Thomas, has contributed the Foreword.

Hardcover: ISBN 9780952206477. Paperback: ISBN 9781908878007. 166 pages.

Dead Woman Walking
By Jessica Mann

Gillian Butler moved away from Edinburgh 50 years ago, or so her friends thought. When her murdered body is found, they must try to remember who last saw her alive. Perhaps it was Isabel, now a novelist and people-tracer, or the twice widowed Hannah, or the psychiatrist, Dr Fidelis Berlin, an expert on child abuse, abandonment, abduction and adoption, who had herself been an unidentified infant rescued from Nazi Germany and now hopes to discover her real name at last. Fidelis Berlin and other characters from Mann's earlier books reappear in this tense, gripping tale of vengeance, family ties and the mystery of identity.

Jessica Mann is the author of 21 crime novels and 4 non-fiction books. As a journalist she has written for national newspapers, weeklies and glossy magazines. She is the crime fiction critic of *The Literary Review.* Jessica and her husband, the archaeologist Professor Charles Thomas, live in Cornwall.

"This is a complex and chilling story, with many shifts of perspective and timeframe. The quality of the writing shines out. The question of changing identity is crucial — not just of individuals but of women in British society over the last half-century. Beneath it all is an elegiac note of regret, a sense of wrong choices with long consequences." — **Andrew Taylor, The Spectator**

"As ever with this author, the intelligent (and complex) texture of the novel matches its sheer storytelling nous." — **Barry Forshaw, crimetime.co.uk**

"Engaging, enthralling and hugely entertaining." — **Frank Ruhrmund, Western Morning News**

"There is a very striking climax, but this is also a novel of ideas, about feminism, family and literature ... As you would expect with Jessica Mann, it's a very well-written as well as a poignant book, and I'm delighted to have read it." — **Martin Edwards, Do You Write Under Your Own Name?**

Paperback, 192 pages. ISBN 978 1 908878 06 9.

Cornwall's Historical Wars
By Rod Lyon

Rod Lyon, BBC Radio Cornwall presenter and former Grand Bard of the Gorsedh Kernow, takes the reader on a fascinating journey through the ages, and through the forgotten wars between the Cornish and their old enemies, the English, revealing a history not taught in schools, and one missing from the 'official' history books. From the early wars with the Saxons, through the rebellions of 1497 and 1549, and on to the Civil War, Rod traces the bloody events which helped to shape the culture and national identity of the Cornish people. This book is essential reading for all those who want to learn the truth about Cornwall's hidden history.

Paperback, 112 pages. ISBN 978 1 908878 05 2.

Chinese Whispers
By Andrew Birtles

Dear Reader, you probably know the party game "Chinese Whispers" but if you don't here's what happens. A group of your friends and family get together, someone starts off with a sentence, in this case "Piglets in pyjamas danced on tiptoes round a tree". Then they whisper to the next person who whispers what they heard to the next and so on and so on...

You'll find it changes every time because people don't hear properly what's been said. Oh, and by the way, you'll be the last person to hear the message so listen very carefully while you're reading this book because without you there won't be a final page.

Yours sincerely, Andrew Birtles

P.S. You may be unfamiliar with some of the words used, so brief descriptions have been included to enhance your enjoyment.

Paperback, full colour, 52 pages. ISBN 978 1 908878 09 0.

Dowsing
By Thomas Fiddick

This reprint of a rare and obscure pamphlet, originally published by Thomas Fiddick of Camborne in 1913, details the various experiments which he undertook whilst dowsing for mineral lodes in his native Cornwall, as well as giving a potted history of mineralogical dowsing in the area. It also gives details of his "Dowsing Cone" and instructions for its use. This book is an invaluable resource for those who study or practise the art of rhabdomancy, or for those who wish to learn more concerning the history of mining in Cornwall. Edited and with an introduction by Chris Bond.

"Great stuff! ... fascinating." - Professor Charles Thomas.

Paperback, 44 pages. ISBN 9781908878 10 6.

Cornwall
By Thomas Moule

Thomas Moule's topographical account of Cornwall is taken from the 1838 edition of The English Counties Delineated and is full of detail concerning the seats of the gentry, the monuments in the churches, the history of the parishes and boroughs and the numbers of houses and inhabitants. This fully-indexed edition is a useful source of information for local historians and for those interested in the Cornwall of 170 years ago. The cover of the book features part of Thomas Moule's map of Cornwall taken from the original edition.

Paperback, 186 pages. ISBN 978 0 9522064 6 0.

Godmanstone Blues
By Chris Bond and Andy Paciorek

Defy not the urge to buy! For this book could save your very living soul.

Poetry and prose by Chris Bond, with original illustrations by the acclaimed artist Andy Paciorek.

Paperback, 72 pages. ISBN 978 0 9522064 9 1.

Forthcoming Titles

Windblown and Desolate: The Story of a North Cornwall Parish, 1500-1700
By Stuart A. Raymond
Paperback : ISBN 978 1 908878 14 4.

The Wheal Margaret Adventure: A Calendar of Agents' Reports and Associated Records, 1857 to 1875
By Chris Bond
Paperback : ISBN 978 1 908878 15 1.

See www.cornoviapress.co.uk for further details.